MW01068802

HE WAS MY, HERO, TOO

A NOVEL

BY

JERALD L. HOOVER

Second of a Four-Part Series – The Hero Book Series

Copyright 2018, 2002 by Jerald L. Hoover
Published by JLH 65 Publishing
(A division of Jerald L. Hoover Productions, LLC)

Mount Vernon, New York
ISBN 13: 978-1717437518

ISBN 10:1717437516

Second Edition: November 2018

Book Cover Design: Jennifer Givner/Acapella Book Cover Design
www.Acapellabookcoverdesign
Photo of Jerald L. Hoover on back cover by Andre Joyles
Edited by Ashley Conner/Ash the Editor
www.AshTheEditor.biz
Edited by Eartha Watts-Hicks/www.Earthatone.com
Proofread by Monique Happy/Monique Happy Editorial Services
www.facebook.com/MoniqueHappyEditorialServices

Printed in the United States of America

For my little "hero" and twin …

My son, Jordan

Other Books of *The Hero Books Series*

My Friend, My Hero

A Hopeful Hero

Hoop Hero

www.TheHeroBookSeries.com

FOREWORD

Over the course of my years, I've been impressed with the abilities of those who were able to rise above what many predicted to be their futures. They confounded the so-called experts and overcame the odds.

One of these exceptional people is the author, Jerald LeVon Hoover, who statistically should've failed. He saw a world that chewed up and spit out so many people that he knew and loved. He saw a world desperate and unfeeling, but he also saw a world of opportunity. One that sent a message that all things are possible if you just believe.

After developing a relationship with this young man over time, I discovered that he had the temerity to succeed, to overcome the odds. Jerald Hoover knew the one common message recurrent in so many people's lives—a willingness to humble themselves and chase a spirit. He chose the spirit that fortified his existence. One that enabled him to reach out and make a way for strength and character. He chose a spirit that allowed him to avoid the familiar path of destruction and despair. He chose a spirit that allowed him to climb mountains and see the star of success.

This young spirit has gone back in time and given back by recording his experiences in book form. Perhaps, as we read this book, it will serve to instruct us to live our lives with even more purpose, determination, and direction.

Jerald LeVon Hoover chose a spirit that allowed him to overcome the odds, and he has done this, knowing there will be a better tomorrow.

Ernest D. Davis

Former Mayor of Mount Vernon, N.Y.

A City That Believes

INTRODUCTION

Evolving! Ongoing! Everlasting feelings are the transcending thoughts, energy, and spirits of our elders and ancestors from our community, Mount Vernon, New York, a.k.a. *The City on the Move* and *A City That Believes.* Our elders' and ancestors' transcending voices are crying out, *Yes ... and still I rise!*

Jerald LeVon Hoover expresses his innermost thoughts, emotions, and fears in this literary work. What's also expressed is his love for God, himself, his family, and the community of Mount Vernon. His concerns encompass the social ills that have plagued this community, its parents, and definitely the youth of today and of the past. *Yes ... and still I rise!*

What's intriguing, unique, heartwarming, and fascinating about *He Was My Hero, Too,* and of course, *My Friend, My Hero,* is the setting, Mount Vernon, New York, where Jerald Hoover decided to develop his characters and storyline around an average African American family, surviving and struggling to move forward. Places such as Levister Towers (the projects), Mount Vernon High School, the Southside Boys and Girls Club, and the local churches of Third Street and Sixth and Ninth Avenues, are all landmarks of Mount Vernon.

Those of us who know and are familiar with these places can truly appreciate and understand Jerald's vision. This is an expression that will have an impact on our youth, their families, and their communities, which, incidentally, are still struggling with the same social issues—drugs, alcohol, teenage pregnancy, AIDS, lack of education, unemployment, along with the Basketball Jones. *Yes ... and still I rise!*

Mount Vernon, with a population of over 80,000 within its four square miles, is a great city. Many cultures and ethnic groups have a profound effect on the greatness of this city. Since the beginning of the twentieth century, African Americans, Jews, Italians, and many other cultures have made contributions that stand out. These cultures and ethnic groups exemplify the rich heritage and strong history that Mount Vernon proclaims. I would like to share a few thoughts, praising the contributions of African Americans and their vital roles in the rich heritage of Mount Vernon. I'm not taking away from any other culture or ethic group, because their influence is equally honorable and well-represented.

I am an African American who is very proud of the evolution, growth, and development of our race and the vital roles we've played in the past and present. Today, my deep emotions are driven by the voices of the elders, ancestors, and my experiences as a Mount Vernonite. I often remind people that you can go across this country, and you won't find another city quite like Mount Vernon—a city that can share and boast of a legacy of successful people in every profession, including politics, education, arts, entertainment, sports, medicine, military, literature, clergy, and human services.

You name it, and an African American from Mount Vernon has achieved it. Denzel Washington, a Mount Vernonite and a product of the Southside Boys and Girls Club, while accepting his historic Academy Award, made mention of Mount Vernon. This is something he does often whenever he's interviewed.

The phenomena are that many of these Mount Vernonites were born and raised in Levister Towers—the projects. They graduated from Mount Vernon High School and were also members of the local Boys and Girls Clubs, the Northside and Southside units, as well as the churches in the area. *Yes ... and still I rise!*

There have been four public schools renamed in Mount Vernon for prominent figures. Three were Mount Vernonites, and one, a person from Africa. These schools were renamed from Robert Fulton to Edward Williams, Nathan Hale to Cecil Parker, George Washington to Nellie Thornton, and James Grimes to Nelson Mandela. These successful achievements pay homage to the elders, ancestors, and unsung heroes from the '20s, '30s, '40s and '50s, whose desire was for their children to work hard and grow up to be somebody. A very simple recipe, and guess what? It worked!

In the late '80s, in a book entitled *A Time To Remember,* Larry H. Spruill, H.D., the Mount Vernon historian, documented the first comprehensive study of Mount Vernon African American history with photographs of the Mount Vernon African American community from the late 1800s through the 1980s. Dr. Spruill is one of those Mount Vernonites, like Jerald Hoover, that grew up in the projects. *Yes! Yes! Yes! And still I rise!*

When you become familiar with the setting and get to look at Mount Vernon's history, all ethnic groups included, you will truly understand Jerald Hoover's work as a writer. He has a strong commitment to express his ability in a way that inspires others to take a look at their lives, issues, pressures, and circumstances and still say, *And still I rise!*

I didn't have the opportunity to interact personally and share experiences with Jerald LeVon Hoover as a young man growing up in Mount Vernon. However, I did share experiences with his strong and courageous mother, Hilda Hoover, and several members of his loving and close-knit family. But now, because of the transcending spirits and energy of the past, from families living in the projects, the opportunity has allowed me to get to know Jerald and share in his creative expression. He is carrying out the call of the elders and ancestors from this great city, Mount Vernon.

It is my hope that you will enjoy reading this novel and that you will gain a vivid understanding of its most essential message. *Yes! Yes! Yes!* I rise again, and again, and again, and again! These are the voices of the elders and ancestors. It's through them that we continue to live and grow.

This belief in the oneness of humankind, which I have often spoken about in concerts and elsewhere, has existed within me, side by side with my deep attachment to the cause of my own race. I do not think, however, that my sentiments are contradictory ... there truly is a kinship among us all, a basis for mutual respect and brotherly love.

– Paul Robeson

William "Billy" Thomas

Former Executive Director

Mount Vernon Boys & Girls Club

CHAPTER ONE

From the *Voice of Music* phonograph, silky-smooth Jazz from the legendary John Coltrane's saxophone permeated the room. Simon sat in deep meditation behind the desk in his office at the South Side Mount Vernon Boys & Girls Club, soaking it all in.

Simon, a portly and bearded man with a tinge of gray hair, wore a dark brown velvet warm-up suit, which blended, almost seamlessly, into the colors of his new office, "The Log Cabin," given the sobriquet by club members after he'd had his new digs renovated with all-wood fixtures.

The only portion that wasn't comprised strictly of maple was the Wall of Fame, where Simon kept the snapshots of every athlete that had graced the club's gymnasium who'd gone on to the professional ranks. He also reserved space for each of the club's Hall of Fame honorees.

Simon's focus was abruptly broken by a knock on the door. Simon, alarmed, swirled around to greet his visitor. It was Kirby, sporting shorts, high-top Chuck Taylor Converse sneakers, droopy socks, and with a white towel, draped around his neck. The two gentlemen smiled, then embraced. "Man, I haven't seen you in a month of Sundays," said Simon, the club's program coordinator, while shutting off the music that stirred his soul.

"Yeah, I know. IBM had me in Chicago doing seminars, and I've been dealing with a few things that sort of needed my immediate and absolute attention."

"I can dig it, Mr. Computer Consultant."

"So, how have you been?"

"Me." Simon smiled and patted on his ever-expanding balloon belly.

"I've been making it just fine. You know, another day, another fifty cents."

"You're a trip," Kirby said.

"So," Simon's tone-of-voice shifted, "how's life in White Plains?"

"It's all right, considering. I really don't do too much there, just work and sleep." Kirby took a deep breath. "It's especially hard not seeing Junior and Bennie every day."

Simon pointed to the photo of Kirby's family positioned on his desk. "And what about Kathy, your wife?"

Kirby made an impulsive about-face and shoved his hands into his pockets to jingle change. "Yeah," he moaned. "I almost forgot. Her, too."

"Hang in there. You guys will be all right."

"I think we're headed for divorce court if you ask me."

"Well, no ... I didn't ask you," Simon said with a sly grin. "You'll see. It'll come around. A year's separation after nine years of marriage isn't the end of the world. Just look at it as a refreshment period, a cleansing period."

"Cleansing? Refreshing? I'd say it's more like an emotional enema."

"Enema?"

"I don't know." Kirby shook his head. "Women be buggin'. It's like a light goes off in their head, and they just ... flip! First, they got our rib, now they take our paychecks!"

"Man..." Simon sounded reticent as he picked up the phone. "Simon speaking, can you hold please." He then placed his hand over the receiver to muffle the sound. "You better not go anywhere in public talking that stuff."

"What? About my wife?"

"No, about the ribs and money."

The door swung open as if a hurricane wind had gotten a hold of it. It was Dannon, clad in a white Adidas sweatsuit and matching white sneakers. "I need a ball, Bruh Simon."

"You forget how to knock, man?" Simon said as he was just about to conclude his phone conversation.

"Oh, I apologize, Bruh Simon. Kirby, what's up?"

"Nothing. Yo, boy, how tall are you now?"

"Six-eight."

"It's only been a couple weeks since I last saw you, and you put on two more inches?"

"I don't know. I guess."

Kirby shook his head in astonishment, cogitating on how it felt like just yesterday when he used to give Dannon piggyback rides.

"Whew! And you're seventeen now?"

"Yep, turn eighteen, June 10th."

"I *know* when your birthday is, chump."

Dannon playfully landed an elbow to Kirby's chest. "Well, I gotta roll. Gotta shoot some hoops, keep my jumper tight."

"When's the next game?" Kirby yelled down the corridor.

"Thursday! Big game against New Ro!"

Kirby made his way back into Simon's office. His thoughts drifted to his best friend, Dannon's older brother, Bennett. He thought about how much he still missed him with every passing day. And the thought of how proud Bennett would've been of Dannon, who'd taken over right where he left off—touted as the best basketball player Mount Vernon High School had ever seen.

Dannon had the same lineaments as Bennett. He was tall, lean, and mean. And he had those catcher's mitt-type hands, which allowed him to palm a basketball with just his thumb and ring finger. He wore a real close haircut. The same way Bennett sported his. And although two inches taller and twenty pounds heavier, his strut was almost the same as Bennett's. They had this confident swagger about them on the court that said, *When I'm on top of my game, no one can guard me.*

The one significant difference between them was that Dannon shot left-handed. That was until Dannon, who was so crazy about the way his big brother played, taught himself how to shoot right-handed, which enabled him to shoot deadly accurate from any range with either hand. A feat accomplished by very few who'd ever played the game.

One sportswriter nicknamed him *Idaho*, a colloquialism for potato. The writer cited the various ways of eating the Idaho potato—mashed, chipped, sliced, boiled, baked, and fried—as a comparison to the many facets of Dannon's game. Any time he took to the court, he was simply a man among boys, a king amongst kings, a lord among—well, maybe not quite that, but you get the idea. Simply put, the young man was awesome.

So much had changed since their days in high school—the town, the people, the school, just about everything. Seemingly, there was nothing in its proper place.

The town of Mount Vernon had elected its first Jewish mayor, a former high school classmate, Sol Weiss. Sol, once class nerd, turned efficacious politician, was also happily coupled with an African American woman.

But drugs had besieged the old neighborhood. Crack, angel dust, heroin, you name it. Young people—ten, eleven, and twelve years old—were committing heinous crimes.

The wholesomeness that was once a trademark of the suburban town just ten miles north of New York City had given way to neglect, disregard for life, and hopelessness. Not to anyone's surprise, some of the local dailies began calling Mount Vernon, *Little Columbia*.

"What happened to this place?" Kirby asked, perusing the pictures.

"What, the club?"

"No," Kirby shook his head and squinted as if he were fending off sunlight, "this city."

"Well ..."

"I was born and raised here. My mother is still here. My wife and kids—"

"Listen, Kirby," Simon said affirmatively. "Times change, people change. I mean, if anyone is an authority on the subject, it's definitely me."

Simon's own metamorphosis was an affirmation. He'd gone from being a numbers-runner, dope pusher, and pimp to being an upstanding, well-respected elder of the community. One who'd become a loving, faithful husband and a devoted stepfather.

Of course, as Simon would tell it, all of that wouldn't have been possible if he hadn't found Jesus Christ as his Lord and personal savior. During that time, he served those five years behind bars. To which end, after his release, Simon answered what he'd perceived as his calling and became an ordained, fire-and-brimstone Baptist preacher.

Simon also met his soul mate, TyDixie, through the Adopt a Prisoner pen pal program, sponsored by her church. At the time, she was a nurse and a single mother of one daughter.

TyDixie was a ravishing woman with huge dimples and short, salt-and-pepper hair.

She had the prettiest hazel eyes that blended nicely with her lightly freckled skin. She was tall with very long legs. In high heels, she towered over Simon and everyone else for that matter. But he couldn't care less, because he knew that as beautiful as she was, it was only a benefit to look up to her.

Simon's noble character also gave birth to a new nickname, Bruh Simon, by many of the locals who'd cited his tireless work with wayward youths as well as adults. He developed and funded a program, Brotherhood Night, a lecture and discussion held every Wednesday at the Boys & Girls Club. Women were permitted, just not encouraged. But they came anyway.

"Why don't you come out to Brotherhood Night tomorrow?"

Kirby, who was shooting paper balls into the trash can, pretending he was his favorite NBA player, Magic Johnson, unleashed a deep sigh. "I don't know."

"Come and bring the boys. They'll enjoy it."

"You still tell those corny jokes at the end of each meeting?"

"Some things never change. And besides, my jokes aren't corny, thank you."

"Yeah, yeah."

"Man, are you all right?"

"Yeah, I'm fine."

"Why are you holding your head? You're still getting those headaches, aren't you? You better get yourself checked out."

"Please, Simon, change the subject. Tell me a joke or something."

Simon dramatized as if a beam of light had just shone upon him, snapped his fingers, and said, "You just reminded me. I have a good one to tell you. This is a real knee slapper."

"My headache is gone now ... see?"

"Sit down."

"Oh, brother." Kirby sat and braced himself as if he was sitting in a spacecraft, awaiting takeoff.

"Two preachers, Reverend Smith and Reverend Jones, both from relatively small churches, met for their weekly lunch. 'Smitty,' Jones said, 'you look troubled. What's the matter?'

'Well,' Smitty answered, 'it seems my watch is missing.'

'You mean the handsome gold one given to you by the Bishop?' Jones asked.

'Yeah, that one. And what's worse is, I fear someone from my congregation may have taken it, while visiting me. It pains me that there may be someone in my own church who can't be trusted. And I would like to know who.'

'I'll tell you what,' Jones said. 'Here's what you do. Next Sunday, give a sermon on the Ten Commandments—a real fire-and-brimstone one. Then, when you get to *Thou Shalt Not Steal*, look out over the entire congregation. I'm certain you'll be able to spot the guilty person.'

'The following week, the two Revs met for lunch again. 'Smitty,' Jones said, 'I see you got your watch back. So, my suggestion worked?'

'Well, in a way.'

'How do you mean, in a way?

'You see, as I was preaching the Commandments and got to *Thou Shalt Not Commit Adultery*, I suddenly remembered where I'd left it.'"

"You're a sick man, Simon. You're not well."

"Aw, a little humor don't hurt nobody."

Kirby tried to keep himself from guffawing by holding his mouth shut for several seconds, but to no avail.

It had to run its course, akin to coffee heightening the awareness of a tired person.

"How come you don't have your meetings at Grace Baptist?" Kirby asked after coming back to his senses. "It'd be less expensive."

Simon gave the question some thought, smiled, leaned back in his chair, and swirled around. "Because money isn't an issue for me right now. Besides, it would then seem like it's a religious thing, and not community engagement. And more than likely, the Jews wouldn't come. The Catholics wouldn't come, nor would the Episcopalians, Methodist, Pentecostals, Protestants, Muslims, or anyone of any other denomination, for that matter." Simon tapped on his desk. "I want them all here. All are welcomed."

Kirby sat as quietly as possible, wrestling with a mixture of negative feelings—guilt, anger, bitterness, and confusion. With all that going on in his head, he offered, in defense, "Look, I didn't forget where I came from. I'm just—"

"I never ever implied—"

"And I definitely didn't forget I'm Black."

"Now, Kirby, you know I never said—"

"I mean," Kirby shook his head with disapprobation, "Mount Vernon ... this place really gives me the creeps. You know, twelve years ... twelve years have passed, and Bennett's killer hasn't been found yet. I just don't understand it. I don't get it."

"Well—"

"And what's with the incompetent police department?"

"Come on, Kirby," Simon said sympathetically. "Lighten up some. They did the best they knew how. They questioned everybody. Me, especially."

"But he was shot in broad daylight ... broad daylight!"

"Yeah ... I understand how you feel."

Kirby cleaned his spectacles and walked over to examine Simon's wall. "Every time I see this picture of Bennett, it gets to me. I don't know, I just miss my partner. He should be playing, making millions in the NBA, not lying cold in a grave in Valhalla."

"God's will," Simon said.

"Yeah, yeah."

Simon swirled around again, only this time, he got up and joined Kirby. "In a sense, he was my hero, too—somebody I wish I could've been like." Simon patted Kirby on the shoulder and retreated to his seat.

"Hey, Simon, what was with the patch on the eye back then?"

Simon peered over his glasses and offered, "That was my trademark."

Kirby had to laugh at that one, but then he noticed something he hadn't seen before on Simon's wall. "A master's degree in Psychology from Kent State ... Simon Timothy Diamond, class of '69. This is yours, man?"

"That's me."

"But why in the world ..."

"Did I live my life the way I did?"

"Yeah."

"I just lost my way," Simon answered matter-of-factly. "It was the '60s, and as you know, it was a very turbulent time for Black people. You could make an argument that we lost a savior when President Kennedy was gunned down. And you could probably make a case for his brother, Robert, who suffered the same fate. Then, Dr. King was murdered—and that was after Medgar was assassinated, getting shot in the back outside his home.

But then after Dr. King, Malcolm X got assassinated for what he stood for and they murdered him right in front of his wife and baby girls. And after that, a host of other civil rights activists were either jailed, savagely beaten, or killed. I was there at Kent State in '65 when National Guardsmen shot those students who were protesting the Vietnam War on campus. I was within a few feet of one of the students who was shot and killed." Simon peeked out the window and into the cloudy, rain-filled skies. "I just gave up after that. My degrees meant nothing to me."

"Nothing?"

"It meant something in terms of me being the first and only in my family to have gotten so far. But in terms of society and humanity, I just didn't care anymore. I used the gift of being a psychologist for all the wrong reasons. I got men and women to do what I wanted them to do. Whether it was run numbers, push dope, prostitute, they did it. I owned and controlled them."

"Man, Simon."

"Yeah, I was bad ... horrible."

"You were a monster."

Simon picked up an eraser and tossed it in Kirby's direction, but Kirby thought fast and managed to duck out of harm's way.

"But you know something?" Simon offered. "I got them all off drugs and cleaned."

"Really? Get outta here."

"No, really. Believe it or not, all my regular customers, I got them detoxed, and a few of them go to church regularly."

"I can believe it. You do have a way of persuasion about you."

"Yeah," Simon said. "But I couldn't get Bennett hooked. He was a strong young man. Strong."

"He had no choice," Kirby said flatly and stared menacingly at Simon. "I would've killed you both."

"Whoa, Kirby, I'm on your side now."

"I know."

The resurrected Simon allowed his emotions to get the better of him as he thought of something in his past. Then he said, "I did lose one. A young sister from my home state, Ohio. She was a nurse, had no family here, made good money, but had it hard growing up." Simon tried to hold back tears, but his resistance was too far down.

Kirby shoved him a wooden tissue box.

"I tried hard to get her cleaned up, but it was too late. She was too far gone, and she died from an overdose." Simon shook his head in disbelief. "Sometimes I wake up in cold sweats. Half the time, I scare my wife half to death because I start crying out the blue."

"Cry, huh?"

"Her name was Wanda. She was a beautiful, God-fearing, Christian girl. I took advantage, and I know her blood is on my hands."

Having it hard was an understatement. Nothing Wanda did was good enough for her parents. She had a younger brother, and her parents seemed to love him more. She had to pay her own way to New York, find her own place to stay, and pay her own way through school by working two jobs.

Her parents—the mother and father from hell—turned deaf ears to an invitation to her graduation. And after they discovered her cause of death, they forbid Simon from having the funeral in his church. The couple arrived in New York, identified the body, and had a rinky-dink ceremony in a funeral parlor. They also refused to take her body back to Ohio, and she was left to be buried in New York.

The two men sat in respectful silence for a time. Simon reminisced regrettably over his past.

His mind also wandered toward an old friend, Willie, who'd served as his driver and bodyguard—his brute in shining armor. Willie was gunned down, shot in the face six times the previous year after answering the cry of a woman being beaten by her boyfriend.

Kirby stared intently at a picture of Bennett dunking on two opponents during their high school championship game. "Simon, I want to find Bennett's killer. I really do."

"You what?"

"I'm serious, man. I want to find out who murdered Bennett in cold blood. I want to know who did that."

"Why? Because you want to kill whoever did it?"

"Right now," Kirby said, giving the question some thought, "the way I feel, I'd kill whoever it is. Tomorrow, on the other hand, after I've slept on it and had a chance to be alone, I probably wouldn't. I just want justice. I want the killer caught."

Kirby walked over to the window and stared out into the abyss.

"But—"

"Simon," Kirby said, snapping his fingers, "you still have connections in the streets, don't you?"

"Of course. I still got peoples."

"Will you help?"

"I'll make a few phone calls. But I think the mayor can help us even more."

Kirby shook his head vigorously.

Simon then added, "You'll have to find the strength to get over it. I know how you feel about him, but he is the mayor, and he may be privy to vital information."

"I don't know about him."

Moments later, Dannon limped into the office. "Bruh Simon, Kirby, I hurt my ankle."

"You all right, man? What happened?" Kirby asked.

"I'm okay." Dannon sat in a chair provided by Simon. "I think I just turned it. I came down on it wrong after goin' up for a dunk."

"Sit tight," Simon said. "Let's have a look at it. Then we'll see if you need to go to the hospital."

As Simon unlaced Dannon's sneaker with Kirby's assistance, Dannon winced in agony, and Simon gave it a once over.

Then Dannon turned to Kirby and smiled. "Why don't you come around the house anymore, Kirby? Momma asks about you all the time."

"It's a long story, Dannon."

"What? You think I won't understand because I'm younger than you?"

"No, it's not that. When I find time—"

"We all know about you and Kathy. We still love you all—you, Kathy, and the kids. I shoot with the boys all the time."

"Okay. Forget that. I'll make time."

"Great. Then you can give me a ride home."

"I *can*?"

"Yeah. You wouldn't want the star of the basketball team walking in the freezing cold with a bum ankle that could stiffen up, would you?"

"Kid," Kirby placed his hand across Dannon's broad shoulder, "you certainly developed your brother's logic."

"Jump shot, too."

The two friends shared a hearty chuckle.

"Hi, honey." The lovely TyDixie elegantly appeared and greeted her husband with a kiss on the lips. In a flash, the office relinquished its stench of sweaty gymnasium odor and gave way to the alluring scent of Chanel No. 5 perfume.

"Hi, Darlin'," Simon said and returned her kiss. "You're just in time. Will you please take a look at Dannon's ankle?"

TyDixie knelt to get a better look at the ankle and said, "Oooh, it's swollen, all right. We'll need some ice."

"Tisha," Simon said through the speakerphone.

"Yes, Bruh Simon."

"Bring me a bucket of ice, please."

"Comin' right up."

Simon snapped his head back in a doubletake at the size of Dannon's foot, then added, "Tisha, I think you better make it a great big bucket of ice."

CHAPTER TWO

Kirby encamped his shiny, black late-model '86, fully loaded 325i BMW in front of Dannon's building. The Levister Tower Housing Project was a ten-story quintuplet of dark brown brick buildings. Each edifice was equipped with an incinerator that blew heavy, dark smoke through the chimney every so often. An intercom system, albeit broken, was installed for security purposes, and it added an element of class. Unfortunately, some of the natives that lived there didn't see it that way and proceeded to destroy it whenever it was in working order.

"Okay, superstar," Kirby quipped. "Why don't you just limp yourself on out of my car."

"Aw, come on. You said you'd come over to see Momma. Besides, you should help me upstairs. You wouldn't want my ankle to suffer any more damage, would you? I mean, not before the big game, right?"

"Of course not, but—"

"No buts," Dannon interrupted and reached over to shut off the ignition. "Too much conjunction use."

"What, are you some type of English literary?"

"Nope."

"Man, you better give me back my keys."

"Not until you say that you'll come see Momma."

As Kirby looked around his old neighborhood, his stomach knotted.

He tried looking at one of his old hangouts—a grassy, diamond-shaped area where he, Bennett, and the rest of his crew used to play their version of baseball.

They were so broke back then that they used a tennis ball and a wooden stick. But his one-time haven had since dried up and was now buried under cement and a razor fence.

Looking around, Kirby gestured to a young woman walking past them into the building. "That young girl there. Isn't she Darlene, Jeff Kendall's baby sister?"

Dannon, massaging his sore ankle, said, "Yeah, all thirteen years of her."

"And she's pregnant?" Kirby said with a bit of annoyance.

"She got knocked up by some drug dealer named Shoo Shoo."

"How old is this Shoo Shoo character?"

"I think around fifteen or sixteen. I know he's younger than me."

"When will these babies stop having babies? When?"

"Man, I wish I could tell you," Dannon said, frowning, thinking the question was for him.

Kirby began frantically patting his pockets, then went into his glove compartment and pulled out his wallet.

"Dannon, you still seeing the girl you introduced me to last year?"

"Diane? Yeah, kinda sorta."

"Well, here. Take this."

"Come on, Kirby, I don't need that."

"Man, the last thing you need right now is a baby.

You're getting ready for college, and you need to only concentrate on your studies and playing ball.

By the way, you ever decide on what school you want to attend?"

"I narrowed my choices down to St. Johns and Syracuse. But—"

Kirby suddenly reverted to the old subject. "It's more than okay to have a girlfriend; but put your priorities first. And don't trust any girl that tells you she's protecting herself. You protect—"

"Kirby, will you please calm down. The reason I don't need one is because I already have one." Dannon went into his bag. "It's as old as can be, but I have it just in case."

"Good for you. Smart man."

"Momma taught me about the so-called birds and the bees. She also warned me. Matter-of-fact, she threatened me." Dannon laughed. "I never knew a little bee could kill a gigantic bird, clip his wings, and have them for a snack."

"Good ole Ms. Wilson. God bless her."

"You can have her."

"Man," Kirby said as he went into reminiscing, "I'll never forget the first time we took Junior to school. After dropping him off at class, Kathy and I had to race to the car so that we could cry in private. It was a very proud moment for us."

"How was Bennie's first day?"

"Oh, Dannon, it was terrible."

"Terrible?"

"Yeah, terrible. We had to drag the little joker out of the car. And once he got into the building, he dropped to his knees, which meant we had to drag him down the hall, kicking and screaming like a madman. I couldn't have cried if I wanted to. I was too worn out."

"That's funny."

"Say, how's your sister?"

Dannon absorbed the random question, then set loose a look of anguish.

"What's the matter? You and Yvette aren't on good terms anymore?"

"It's not me and Yvette," Dannon revealed. "I'm nuts about my big sister. I love her to death. It's her crazy husband and his wacky kids I ain't too thrilled with. I don't know why she married that clown anyway. Not only is he twelve years older than her, he's also been married five times and has seven kids. The youngest two brats live with them."

"How does your Momma feel about him?"

"She's from the South." Dannon waved his hand. "She loves everybody. Always hollerin' to just give him a chance."

"And I guess you aren't willing to do that?"

"Hey, four strikes and you're out—give it up."

"Dannon—"

"Kirby," Dannon interceded, "the last woman he married was a marital counselor *and* relationship expert. You figure that one out."

"I can understand how you feel." Kirby smiled. "But you'll have to find a way to deal with it so that it won't cause a strain between you and Yvette."

"I know, I know."

"As far as relationships go, I'm certainly no expert myself. Just look at me. I'm separated from Kathy, but I do have a theory. It may not be shared by most though. I think of relationships like I think of automobiles—new cars in particular."

"What do you mean?"

"Just think, when a person buys a brand-new car, he or she cares for it like it's a newborn baby. The *new car* smell is intoxicating, and they won't allow anyone to eat in it.

They go to the car wash at the least once a week and stare back at the car with admiration after buffing it. The rides down the bumpiest streets feel smooth, and they practically have to wipe off their feet before they get in.

"Then all of a sudden, the new smell disappears. There may be coins or a French fry or two in the backseat or on the floor. Now instead of washing it once a week, they may only wash it once a month, and that's only if they can find the time. When they hit a bump in the road, not only is it rocky, but it almost feels like an earthquake.

"The monthly note becomes a burden. Then the car suffers its first fender bender or scratch. And don't forget the dreaded mechanical problems. After a while, the automobile has become a headache. But low and behold, after a while, they're riding down the street, and they see another car—a newer, more beautiful car. Something more pleasant and delightful to the eyes, and now they're ready to trade what they have for something else."

"You really feel that way? You think it's really like you said?"

"Think about it. When you meet someone you like, you can't stop thinking about her. The phone can't ring enough. Every day is sunny. Then, when the rain pours, and the winds of war begin to rage, you're ready to jump ship or find someone more appealing."

"You know what they say," Dannon said with a smile, "one man's trash is another man's treasure."

"Man, that only works if you work for the Department of Sanitation."

The two gentlemen exploded into raucous laughter.

"Is that how you feel about marriage too, bruh?"

"Marriage is a little different, especially if there are kids involved. But the principles are the same, and I personally think a lot of people get married because they're tired of dating. Not because true love exists between them."

"Maybe they just fell in love with the wrong people," Dannon insisted.

"Yeah, that's usually the case."

"I think I see your point, though. See ... this is why I want to find the woman of my dreams before I ever get married."

"You'll find the woman of your dreams, all right. Just keep going to sleep. Keep snoozing, she'll be there."

"You tryin' to tell me that the woman of my dreams doesn't exist?"

"No, she exists, but you'll have to keep your eyes wide open to find her. You can't just fantasize about her. Just keep on living, Dannon. Just keep living. But remember, there are no perfect people."

As the temperature began to drop, Dannon could feel goosebumps rise on his arms. He reached for Kirby's watch and said, "We've been in this car for over an hour. Why don't you come upstairs? Come on, please?"

After another mild protest, Kirby gave in.

CHAPTER THREE

Outwardly, Kirby fronted like he had nerves of steel. Inwardly, he felt uneasy, troubled, angry, and confused. Stepping into the building, memories of his past began to grate at him. And at the thought of not having returned to the house that he knew as his second home in over eleven years, his heart raced. He desperately wanted to return to his car.

"How does it smell?" Dannon teased as they stepped into the elevator.

"All too familiar."

Dannon amusingly took a whiff of the urine odor. "You kinda get used to it."

"Will you just press the button?"

Soon, the journey with an odor more powerful than smelling salts was over.

Once inside the apartment, Dannon turn to Kirby and said, "Wait here." He limped to the back room. "Momma! You home? I have a surprise for you."

Kirby sat in the trophy-occupied living room, which was once Bennett's bedroom. A lot had changed since his last visit. Bennett's former bedroom was laden with a new matching leather sofa and loveseat. There were two glass end tables with lamps on them and a coffee table that had an Oriental rug under it. And the wall was decorated with African paintings.

Kirby spotted a photo album on the coffee table. A picture of the 1973 Mount Vernon High School basketball team. That team, led by Bennett, captured Mount Vernon's first and only New York state championship.

A brand-new stove and refrigerator, provided by Housing, occupied the kitchen. Tasteful floral placemats and a bowl of plastic fruit dressed up the beautiful, brown eating table, serving as the centerpiece of the dining area.

I wonder where those guys are now? Kirby asked himself, thinking of his teammates. He knew the fate of his beloved best friend, and he knew about himself—the guy who used to tell jokes while riding the bench.

Big Joe Hancock, the starting center, went on to play college ball at the University of Florida and got drafted by the Boston Celtics. His brief NBA career ended fast. When he pulled a hamstring right after training camp, they cut him. He decided to play professional ball overseas, in Italy for big bucks.

Dexter Stratton, the Bennett clone but only four inches shorter, attended Iona College, the school Bennett was going to attend, received his degree in English, and was now teaching at Mount Vernon High School. He married his college sweetheart and had one daughter. Dexter still kept in touch with Kirby on a daily bsasis.

Ronnie O'Koren graduated high school and became part owner of a gas station. Davey "Honey Jack" Sanchez moved to California and didn't leave a contact number. John "Great White Hope" Berry took over his parents' bakery after being dishonorably discharged from the Army.

Jeffrey Bryce Frazier got strung out on heroin after returning from Vietnam and walked around all day, dribbling and shooting an invisible basketball. Brandon "Petty Cash" Jones died in Vietnam. Stanley "K" Rowinsky, the guy whose legs formed the letter "K" whenever he stood still, wasn't doing much with his life these days. He was divorced, unemployed, and had three kids. He just lived every day as it came.

Jeffrey Kendall became a background singer for television commercials. And Hezekiah "The Preacher" followed in his father's footsteps after graduating from Howard University's Divinity School. He became the pastor of Metropolitan Baptist Church in New Rochelle. Folks now called him "Rev. Doc."

"Kirby." Dannon interrupted Kirby's thoughts. "Momma will be out in a minute."

"Was she asleep? Did you wake her up? If so, I don't want to disturb her. I can leave."

"You trying to get me killed? She hasn't seen you in years. You haven't been here since Bennett died, and you think—"

Kirby held up his hand. "I understand."

"Thank you."

While continuing to look through the photo album, Kirby came across a picture of Bennett holding baby Dannon.

"Do you ever feel pressure from being Bennett's younger brother?"

Dannon pondered the question and smiled. "Yeah, sometimes. But it's a good kind of pressure. More of a pathway. I think if he were alive, I'd feel more pressure, but now I kinda feel like he's just watchin' over his baby brother, and I'm comfortable with that. I wish he was still here though. I miss my big brother a lot."

"I know the feeling all too well."

"To make me feel better, Momma used to tell me about a story of Elisha and Elijah in II Kings of the Bible. How when Elijah went away to Heaven, he really didn't taste death. He just went up in a flaming chariot, and afterwards, Elisha took over for him. Elisha used to be just like I was with Bennett, following Elijah around. I kinda try to feel the same way, too. Like Bennett's not really dead, just in Heaven resting or something."

"Your Momma and the Bible."

"Ain't she a trip though? I mean, she has a G.E.D., but before that, only an eighth or ninth grade education. Nevertheless, she's probably read every book published, and the woman knows the Good Book like the back of her hand."

"That's what you call mother wit, Dannon."

"Mother *what*?"

"Kirby, my sweetie." Ms. Wilson entered the room, wearing a blue flannel nightgown. She hadn't changed much since Kirby last saw her. She still had a chubby build and a healthy head of gray hair. The high blood pressure that once troubled her so much, only flared occasionally. Now that she worked at City Hall in the mayor's office, she worked day hours instead of a hectic nightshift, standing on her feet in a factory.

"Ms. Wilson."

"Well, how have you been? Come here and give me a hug, son."

"I've been doing fine. It's good to see you," Kirby said during the clinch.

"You look just wonderful. How's Kathy and the boys? Would you like somethin' to eat?"

"No, thank you, and everybody's doing just fine. And yourself?" Kirby asked as he pulled away.

"Oh, Momma's doin' just fine. You know I'm workin' with the mayor now."

"So I've heard." Kirby sat down. "Ms. Wilson, I don't mean to be disrespectful or to pry into your business, but I can't stand the guy. How can you work for him?"

"Momma," Dannon interrupted, "I'm goin' to my room to soak my foot and do my homework. Kirby, I'll see you at the club."

Ms. Wilson sat beside Kirby and placed her hand on his. "You'll have to find a way to get over it."

"But, he married Tara."

"Son, Bennett is gone. Tara is free to marry whomever she pleases."

After reasoning with it, Kirby reluctantly lamented, "Yeah, I guess you're right, but I still don't like it. She should've married Bennett, that's all."

"I know how you feel. But don't hold grudges, baby. It's ungodly."

"Ms. Wilson, I don't like him, but now I may have to enlist his help in finding Bennett's killer."

"What you say, Kirby?"

"Oh, I'm sorry, Ms. Wilson."

"What's going on?"

"Ms. Wilson, I want to find Bennett's killer. It's been twelve years, and no one, I mean no one has been brought to justice. I don't get it."

"I was angry, bitter, and confused myself, but I put it all in God's hands, and I'm trying to let go. Whoever killed my baby will have to pay their debt sooner or later."

"I know, but—"

"Listen, Kirby, when I lost Bennett, I lost my life. He was my firstborn. I cried something terrible, and I seriously thought I was gonna die. Kirby, I never thought I'd have to bury my own son. It's a dreadful experience for a parent to bury their child. But I knew I had to find the strength to go on for Yvette's and Dannon's sake. Many days and nights, I prayed and asked God to heal my pain."

"Ms. Wilson—"

"You know something ..." Ms. Wilson grabbed Bennett's graduation picture off of the end table. "Lord, Bennett gave me the hardest time. I was in so much pain giving birth to that boy. But once I saw him in that incubator, I knew in my heart he was going to be something special. Sometimes we have to just accept God's will, trust Him, and move on as best we can."

"Simon said the same thing ... in a roundabout way. I miss my boy, Ms. Wilson, my brother, and I want justice."

"I understand. So, what are you gonna do?"

"Well ..." Kirby contemplated for a moment, then answered, "I asked Simon for help with his street contacts. You know, to see what they can come up with. And I guess I'll go to the police or whoever it takes to get the job done."

"Good luck, honey. I wish you all the luck in the world, and I'll be prayin' for you day and night. But be careful. Be very careful. You still have a family to raise, and they need you here and healthy."

Kirby got up to shake off the aggravation and to investigate the family pictures. Just as he got to the wall unit, he ran across his absolute favorite—the one with him and Bennett.

JUNE 1973

Kirby pinched his best friend's hand as he laid stone-still in a hospital bed, hoping by some miracle that he'd squeeze back. Fearful, Kirby felt his heart flutter as his mind began to race a million miles a minute. He wished he was a doctor, a genie, or some miracle worker that could reverse the hands of time, and thus, have the power to change the outcome of whatever he pleased.

Kirby's biggest nightmare came to pass, and he lost total control of his emotions. The deafening sound of the expired life pack permeated throughout the hospital room. Kirby's eyes were blinded by the flow of uncontrollable tears.

All of a sudden, there was a clamorous crash, and a trampling sound, akin to a herd of raging bulls, grew louder. Kirby looked up while his head was laid upon Bennett's chest and noticed that Bennett was being bum-rushed by a team of nurses and a doctor.

Kirby was pulled up and away by a gentle nudge from one of the nurses. His eyes fixated on Bennett, whose only bodily function was the reaction to the defibrillator shock. Kirby, realizing the end was imminent, made his way over to the priest who stood outside the room with a Bible in tow.

"Father," Kirby said through the rush of tears, "is there anything you can do for my boy?"

The priest, who was a stumpy fellow with white hair and black, thick glasses, peered inside the room and checked on the doctor and nurses working frantically to revive Bennett. Then he placed his hand on Kirby's shoulder and smiled. "Son, it's in the Lord's hands now. All we can do is hope, pray, and keep faith."

"I don't think I know what that means, Father."

Just as Kirby was about to offer an imploration for more help, the head doctor approached them with a sullen look.

"No!" Kirby shrieked at the top of his lungs.

The doctor looked at the priest, then to Kirby and shook his head. "I'm sorry."

Kirby exploded away and went in the direction of Bennett, only to be held back by nurses.

"No! You gotta do somethin'!"

"Young man." The priest got a hold of him. "I know you're hurting, but you have to compose yourself."

The head doctor tapped Kirby on the shoulder as a show of support and then walked off, mentioning that he had to call Bennett's mother.

Kirby took another glance over at Bennett, who by this time was fully covered with the bed sheet. Upon seeing this, Kirby snapped. He yelled, raced down the corridor, and onto the stairwell. He reached the lobby in no time, and that's where he met up with Big Joe and Dexter.

"Kirby! What's wrong, man!" a frightened Dexter asked.

"It's Bennett, Dex! He's gone, man! Gone! Gone for good!"

The three companions formed a circle to console and comfort one another.

"I'm gonna get whoever did this," Kirby said, trying to get himself together. "I'm gonna make whoever did this pay dearly. I'm gonna do him!"

"K-K-Kirby, l-l-let th-th-th—"

"I'm not tryin' to hear nothin' you have to say, Joe, about lettin' the law handle it. Look at how long it's been already. It's been weeks! I'm gonna do it my way. Are you guys with me or what?"

A peep couldn't be heard from either man. Only looks of bewilderment and distress.

"We have to be strong for Bennett's family," Dexter said. "But you, especially."

"Don't tell me what I gotta be, Dex!" Kirby said, pointing a finger in Dexter's face. "I've been comin' here nonstop for six weeks. Don't tell me nothin' about bein' strong. Where were you? Huh? Huh?"

"Kirby what's wrong with you?"

"Ye-ye-yeah, wh-wh-what's th-th-the matter?"

Kirby served his two friends an expression of disgust before storming off, exclaiming, "I'll handle this my own way! I'll do it myself! I don't need no fair-weather friends no way!"

"Kirby." Dexter chased after him, only to get caught and held back by Big Joe.

"Le-le-let him g-g-go. He'll b-b-be fine af-af-after 'while."

As Kirby stormed down the sunny streets of Mount Vernon, he wore a look of rage and confusion. His best friend, his buddy, was gone, shot to death like an animal. So many unanswered questions traveled in and out of his head. *Why couldn't the police find who did it? Why would someone kill Bennett? Why would someone just shoot him in broad daylight with so many people around? Who would want to shoot him at all?*

Kirby unhesitatingly decided that he'd break the news to Tara. He reached her house and attempted to compose himself by taking a few deep breaths before ringing the doorbell.

Mr. Copeland, Tara's father, opened the door and greeted Kirby with his usual, "What's up, Slick?"

Kirby exchanged greetings, then made his way through the foyer, into the living room, and took a seat directly across from Mrs. Copeland. Once eye contact was made, Kirby told the story. Then he dropped his head in anguish and burst into tears.

Mrs. Copeland uttered, "Dear Lord," and proceeded upstairs to get Tara.

When Tara arrived downstairs, she and Kirby embraced.

"Tara," Kirby said, reinforcing his grip around her waist. "He's gone, Tara. He's gone."

"It's gonna be all right, Kirby. Everything will be all right. We have to hold on. We're gonna to have to be strong." Tara broke away and took a seat on the couch to collect her thoughts. "Kirby, we have to be strong for everybody, including ourselves."

Kirby sat beside her. "I know, Tara, but I have so much anger inside me. I can't understand this. I can't at all. I don't know what to think, and with no arrest or anything ..."

Tara sucked in a deep breath and released it slowly. "I know. I don't understand that either. But this is where our faith in the justice system as well as our faith in God has to come in."

"I'm sorry, Tara, but when it comes to religion ... you know I'm not the most—"

"Well, you have to dig deep for some inner peace now or—"

Kirby got up and paced the room. Then he grabbed the glass of tea that Mrs. Copeland had brought for him. "I'm going to kill whoever did this!"

"Kirby, please, for goodness sake, don't start talking like that. It's insane! You'll go to jail!"

"Why do you think I'll get caught?" Kirby said matter-of-factly. "They didn't catch the person who shot Bennett. I probably have more suspects than they do."

"Kirby, you can get yourself killed. Do you honestly think Bennett would want that? Please let the police handle it."

Just as Kirby was about to react with more frustration, Tara's parents re-entered the room. Mr. Copeland sat next to Tara and placed his arm around her, while Mrs. Copeland stood by Kirby and gently rubbed his back.

"Well," Mrs. Copeland said, "I've just spoken with Ms. Wilson."

"How is she?" Tara's interest piqued. "I have to get over there."

"She's okay." Mrs. Copeland took a seat. "She's home with Kirby's mother."

"Good, she's not alone," Tara replied.

"She, of course," Mrs. Copeland continued, "just wants us all to pray for her and the rest of the family."

"Mrs. Copeland," Kirby said with a bit of annoyance in his voice, "I don't mind all the prayin' and stuff, but shouldn't we be out lookin' for the creep or creeps who shot Bennett? I mean ..."

CHAPTER FOUR

It was a sweltering summer day, with temperatures hovering around the century mark. The date was June 18, 1973. The day the city of Mount Vernon said goodbye to one of its most honorable sons. Hundreds of family members and friends jammed into Macedonian Baptist Church. The red-brick, two-story church sat in the middle of Ninth Avenue, between Second and Third Street.

While scores of despondent family members and friends were inside, what seemed like thousands of well-wishers lined the streets around the church to pay their last respects to the young basketball legend.

Bennett lay in an open, oversized brown casket to accommodate his muscular six-foot-six-inch frame, dressed in his basketball uniform amid flowers and a memorial from classmates. His mother sat next to him, clutching a baby photo of him.

The pastor, Reverend Henry Ewault, was kind enough to honor the family's request and have speakers outside for those who couldn't get in. It appeared the whole city was in attendance, and the media coverage was enormous. Every newspaper within the tri-state area was there. TV camera crews were set up inside and outside.

Many of the so-called important people took their turns paying tribute. Even the governor sent condolences by way of telegram. The service was so emotionally charged that whenever a well-wisher stepped down from the podium after speaking or singing, they left in tears or filled with the Holy Ghost. One song, *Soon We'll Be Done with the Trouble of This World*, sung by Sister Lisa Jackson–Stone, tore into the hearts of many.

Newly appointed Principal of Mount Vernon High School, Mildred Cummings, was one of the first to speak. Principal Cummings, as she fancied to be called, was a slender woman and very elegant.

She always wore these big hoop earrings and a powerfully fragrant perfume.

She gave a riveting speech that struck a major chord with everyone. But it was what she said towards the end that made everyone want to check themselves.

"Some, if not all of us, may be asking, why did this happen? Bennett was only eighteen years old, and he was such a sweet guy. Why did he die? But the real question we should ask ourselves is, why did he live?"

She paused for a moment and looked over the congregation. "Folks, your answer is right in front of you. Your answer is right beside you. Your answer is right behind you. Look at us, we're a mass of people, sitting sorrowfully but sitting peacefully. We're comforting one another. We're supporting one another. But most of all, as presently constituted, we're different races, different religions, different sexes, and we're still showing love for one another. This is a celebration of humanity. Bennett, my friend," she said and smiled at the body. "You brought us all together in a very special way. Sure, today we come in sadness, as we should. But today, we also come to honor you. Thank you for bringing us together."

Principal Cummings received loud responses of "Amen" from those who agreed with her. "And we should all search inside and challenge ourselves to sustain this love we've shown toward one another in this trying time. There's a war going on. People are dying unnecessarily over there in Vietnam. But there's a war going on right over here on American soil. It's called racism. And it's alive and well at almost every turn. Let us pray and try to put an end to all this madness. Let's do it, one for all.

I'm not saying give up your cultures, but let's see if we can come together as a people. One people. Let's celebrate humanity."

"Bennett," she said and turned to the casket a second time, "thank you for giving voice to the concerns that face our youth. You know, dear hearts, this young man was totally against drugs. He was totally against succumbing to peer pressure. He wanted young people to enjoy life to the fullest. He was very much for education and liberation. He was only eighteen years old, but he was on our side, folks. He was on our side. Oh, Bennett ... dear, dear, Bennett. Sleep on and take your rest, for we loved you dearly, but our Creator in Heaven loved you best."

Everyone seemed to stand in unison and pound their hands together loudly. The ovation lasted for nearly five minutes, and that included the folks outside. Later, she told the reverend that speaking for so long wasn't in her plans, but something had grabbed a hold of her tongue and she couldn't stop. Like a spirit, a pleasant and comforting spirit, was urging her to testify on Bennett's behalf.

When Reverend Ewault, a bronze-colored, stout man with a full dark beard that matched the little hair he had left on his head, did the eulogy, he sang *'Till We Meet Again*. He then reflected on his time with Bennett. He relayed that he knew God's will had been done, but personally, he was grieving.

"Bennett, I know you're in a better place. I just feel that in my heart. Your friends, family, and loved ones, we'll all miss you. You left us too soon. We wish you could've given us just a little more time to love you. But we thank you for coming into our lives."

Kirby sat next to his mother, Lois, on the second pew with the rest of the Wilson family and received comfort.

Bennett's family members consisted of his mother, his sister, Yvette, his brother, Dannon, Tara, who sat between her parents, and Aunt Traci. Also accounted for were a host of cousins, aunts, uncles, and his godparents.

Albeit a sad day, everything appeared to go exceptionally well.

That was until it came time to view the body, when a loud outburst shook everyone.

"Get away from me! I'm trying to get to the body!" shouted an enraged man who appeared to be unbalanced. He was dressed in a wrinkled black suit, a dirty white shirt, and a ruffled black tie. He also wore a wide-brimmed hat that covered most of his forehead. His walk was very unsteady, which explained why his shoes were so run over. "I want to know who killed him! I want justice!" He continued wobbling down the middle aisle toward the casket.

"Mister, please," said a male usher, who winced and turned his head to fight off the horrible smell, "this is a funeral. Have some respect. You can't just come down the middle aisle like that. If you want to view the body, you'll get your chance like everyone else. Please go outside and wait your turn."

In a huff, the man snatched his arm away from the usher and said, "Move outta my way, boy. Who killed him! Who shot him!"

"Ushers! Ushers!" Reverend Ewault shouted.

"Betty," the man said to Ms. Wilson as he approached her and removed his hat to fully reveal himself. "Who killed our son? Who shot our boy?"

Ms. Wilson was so overcome with shock that she fainted and had to be carried out.

Unfortunately, the commotion didn't stop there. Ms. Wilson's sister, Traci, was known to have a bad temper and showed no signs of having changed. She was a heavyset woman with jet black hair that went down to her shoulders, and she had real big hands that made for cast iron fists. After she gathered herself and reared back, she uncorked a punch that sent the man sprawling to the floor, where he laid in a comatose state.

He was the same man who'd vanished five years prior without a trace.

CHAPTER FIVE

Kirby reversed to make eye contact with a grim-faced Ms. Wilson, who was sitting on the couch.

"I think I'll be heading home now," Kirby said. "I have an early day tomorrow. Man, my head is killing me."

Ms. Wilson got up and place her hand on Kirby's shoulder. "Don't stay away so long. I know you see Dannon at the Boys & Girls club, but Momma wants to see you sometimes."

"I'll try, Ms. Wilson. I'll try."

"Listen, you're gonna have to find a way to get over your pain. Find a way to move on."

"Ms. Wilson, the only way I'll probably get over this bitterness is if Bennett's murderer is either put in jail or the grave."

Taken aback by Kirby's last elucidation, Ms. Wilson responded, "Kirby, son, that don't sound at all like you. I can only imagine how difficult and frustrating it must be, but you have to realize that things will work out in their own time. And as I said before, Bennett's killer will have his day before the Lord. You can count on it."

"Not if I get to him first."

"Kirby—"

"I'm sorry, Ms. Wilson, but I'll have to work on it."

"I'll be praying for you and your family."

"Thank you," Kirby said, then kissed Ms. Wilson on the cheek and left the apartment, taking one of Bennett's trophies.

******

No sooner had Kirby put his key in the door than the telephone rang. It was rare that he ever felt like talking to anyone, but he forced himself to answer it.

"Kirby?"

"Hey, Simon, what's up?" Kirby popped a pill in his mouth and collapsed into his reclining chair.

He'd rented a one-bedroom dwelling in the posh section of White Plains, which sat twelve miles north of his hometown and was considered the most metropolitan city in Westchester County. He had all the modern appliances and conveniences. Plush, wall-to-wall carpeting, washer and dryer, a frost-free refrigerator, and customized ceiling fans in every room. The flat was armed with a garbage disposal and microwave oven. The intercom system was state-of-the-art—you could see the caller on a fifteen-inch monitor imbedded in the wall.

"Got news for you. Sort of, anyway."

"Yeah." Kirby squinted while applying pressure against his head with a warm rag. "What's up?"

"Well, you asked me if I still had contacts, right?"

"Yeah," was Kirby's response again, only this time with more excitement. He sat up straight. "What'cha got?"

"I got a hold of an old buddy of mine, Harry Hooch. He just got out of prison. He may know a few people. He's gonna make a few calls, then get back to me probably tomorrow or Thursday, the latest."

"Man, that's great. Fantastic. Where do we go from here?"

Simon, ever the deliberate one these days, added, "Not so fast. Let's just wait and see what Hooch has to say. He may have something, or he may not have anything at all."

"Let's hope he has plenty."

"I have faith in him. If there's anything out there, he'll find it for us."

"Solid!"

"So, I'll see you and your boys at Brotherhood Night tomorrow, right?"

"I don't know about that one."

"You want help from me, don't you?"

"Aw, Simon, don't go there on me."

"Hey," Simon said affirmatively, "one good turn deserves another. I'll see you tomorrow."

"Yeah, Simon," Kirby blew into the air. "Okay."

"Goodnight, my friend. Oh! By the way, I have another—"

"Joke? Simon, do I have to?"

"Yes, just listen. This guy's wife died, and after the funeral, the grief-stricken husband rode back in the limo with his best friend. The friend was trying desperately to comfort his sobbing main man. The best friend said, 'Larry, one day, maybe not soon, but not too far off either, this will all pass. No ... not the memory of your wife, your confidant, your lover, your soul mate, but all this pain. And someday, maybe even sooner than you think, someone else will come along, not to replace your wife, but to fill a void in your life. She'll be more than willing to share that time with you. And one of these days, I promise you, you'll find her, and you'll have a full and enriching life again. One day, she'll be there.'

Larry stopped crying, looked at his friend, and said, 'Yeah, I understand all that, but ... but what am I gonna do about tonight?'"

Simon, after an extended crack-up, called out to Kirby. "How's that? Did you like that one? Kirby? Kirby? Kirbster ... Kirb ... Kirby ..."

CHAPTER SIX

JUNE 1973

"Dust to dust, ashes to ashes," Reverend Ewault said while crushing a flower over Bennett's coffin, as the undertakers laid him to eternal rest.

Overall, there had to be more than one hundred cars that followed the procession from the church in Mount Vernon to the cemetery in Valhalla, New York, some twenty miles away, and to keep the travel flowing smoothly, state troopers closed down the northbound side of Interstate 287.

Bennett's gravesite was on a hill overlooking a dam of water. Kirby, who was attired in a black pinstriped suit, stood alongside the rest of the basketball team. Dannon tugged away at Traci's side, while Yvette unsuccessfully tried to comfort her mother.

Kirby glanced at Dexter, who was standing beside him, wearing a brown suit and dark shades. "I'm gonna get whoever did this."

"Le-le-let the po-po-police ha-ha-handle it, K-K-Kirby," Big Joe advised.

"He's right, man. Let the police handle it. We're all upset over this, but let them handle it. We keep tellin' you this. Play it safe. Hey, whoever killed Bennett is obviously still out there. He or they must be dangerous. Let the police handle it."

Kirby looked Dexter straight in the eye and deadpanned, "I am the police. I'll find them and bring them to my own justice."

Big Joe, who'd recently chopped his afro and added ten pounds of muscle, making him a beefed-up six-foot-eight and 250 pounds, began to get nervous. As he attempted to speak, he patted his foot and slapped his thigh. Nothing would come out until he was able to settle down.

"K-K-Kirby, be careful."

"I will be. I will be."

******

"Son, where are you going?" Kirby's mother, Lois, asked from her seat at the kitchen table.

Lois was a young-looking forty-something and brown-skinned. Her face was sprinkled with tiny moles. She was slender and petite, and she, like the rest of the women in her family, had hips the size of Texas.

It was alleged that once, when Lois was crossing a busy street in downtown New York City, wearing tight blue jeans, she caused a nine-car accident because a driver failed to take his eyes off her. And guys from the neighborhood would joke with Kirby, telling him, *"Pam Grier ain't got nothin' on your Moms!"*

"I'm going out for a walk. I need some air."

"It's almost midnight, and it's raining like crazy out there. Kirby, do you need to talk? Son, you can talk to me."

"I know, Momma, I know. But I just ... I just need to get some air. I'll be back shortly, I promise." Kirby kissed his mother's forehead. "Don't wait up for me though."

"You bet I'll wait up. Here, take my umbrella."

Seconds later, Kirby was out trekking the darkened and drenched streets of Mount Vernon. Where he was going, he didn't know, but he walked and walked and walked. His travel took him to a place where he stumbled across Simon. Simon was standing outside the Dew Drop Inn bar with his companion, Willie, and another man holding a cane.

Kirby quickened his strut and purposely brushed Simon with his shoulder.

"Excuse me, young fella," Simon said after the mysterious hit.

"Man, if I find out you had anything to do with my friend's murder ... I promise, I'll kill you! You understand me!"

Kirby was collared before he could bat an eye.

"Whoa, Willie, he's just a kid. Just a kid. Let him go. It's all right."

"I'll show you how much of a kid I am. I'll shove that umbrella down your throat!"

"You better quit while you're ahead," Willie demanded.

"It's cool, Willie." Simon flashed a smirk. "Now, now, young fella. First off, I had nothing to do with Bennett's murder. I was out of town on business when it happened."

"Like you couldn't get somebody to do your dirty work. Like one of your dope fiend flunkies."

"Murder isn't my game. Never has been, never will be."

"What do you call that mess you push on the streets."

"Feel Good," Simon said, laughing, and high-fived Willie.

"I'll show you *feel good*," Kirby countered and dropped Simon with a right to his jaw.

Willie charged Kirby and lifted him up over his head. Just as he was about to slam his body to the pavement, Simon rose to his feet and said, "Let him go, Willie." He put his rain-soaked hat back on.

"But Simon, he just—"

"Turn him loose! Now, I said!"

"You're lucky, kid." Willie gathered himself and picked up his umbrella.

"This ain't over, Simon! You too, Bubba!"

Simon stood amidst the weighty downpour and watched Kirby as he stormed down the street.

Willie walked over to his boss and handed him a handkerchief. "You okay? You want me to break him up once and for all?"

With his eyes still affixed on Kirby, Simon wiped the blood from his mouth. "No, don't hurt him. As a matter of fact, I want you to protect him."

"Say what?"

"You heard me." Simon shoved the bloody handkerchief into Willie's chest. "I want him protected. You guys are responsible for his safety. See to it nothing happens to him."

"Boss," Willie said, "I don't understand."

"There's a thing called friendship, and that kid lost his best friend. He's got a lotta heart, that youngun'. He cared about his boy. That's loyalty. I like that."

"Who do you think could've done it?" asked Little Tiny Smalls. Little Tiny Smalls was a huge man. He had to be at least 360 pounds. He had this great big water tank head and the biggest hands. And the walking cane wasn't for walking. Tiny Smalls didn't have a limp or a bad leg. The cane was used to crack heads.

"You got me, Tiny. I didn't hear anything about a contract out on him. Who knows, it could've been out-of-towners."

"But," Willie jumped in, "who'd want to kill a high school ball player like that? I mean, he was Bennett. How many enemies could he have had?"

"Listen," Simon said just as he was about to get into the backseat of his navy blue, white-walled Caddie, "I want you to put a tail on him. Nothing obvious. A light tail. He just lost his buddy, but at the rate he's going, he'll soon be joinin' him. Don't let anything happen."

"I'll get right on it," Tiny Smalls said. "I'll go inside and make a few calls."

******

"Kirby, you're soaked." Tara was clad in a pink flannel nightgown with a matching robe and oversized Bugs Bunny slippers. "Whew! You're drunk, too. Come on inside. It's pouring out." Tara, who was also grieving and confused, had managed to keep her runway model looks intact.

"I know it's late, but I need to talk to someone." Kirby staggered inside.

Tara's family had the biggest and prettiest house on the block. But they were constantly changing its color. Whatever the mood was for Tara's father, that's the color he chose. The outside was painted lavender, trimmed in purple.

"Sure, it's not a problem. I understand."

"You weren't asleep, were you?"

"No," Tara took Kirby's unopened umbrella away from him. "I was just sitting here with Sol, discussing plans for college, is all."

"Sol? What's he doin' here?"

"Kirby."

"Where is he?" Kirby said and stormed past her.

Sol overheard the commotion and sat nervously at the dining room table in front of a cup of hot chocolate.

"Kirby, come here!"

Kirby snatched Sol's hat and raincoat and mashed them against his sternum.

"Tara, what's up?" Sol asked.

"Hey, man, what're you doin' here this time of night? Bennett just died. What's up with this?"

As Sol began to say, "You wouldn't hit a guy with glasses on, would you?" Kirby swung.

The first punch missed and missed badly. The second punch seemed to come all the way from South America and knocked him silly.

It took Sol a moment to realize Kirby had knocked him off his feet. As if by instinct, Sol immediately began searching for his glasses while scrambling to get to himself upright. He managed to tell Tara, "I'll see you some other time. I'm outta here!"

Kirby went after Sol again, but Tara moved quickly to intervene and pushed him back, saying, "Kirby, are you crazy? What's wrong with you?"

"Honey," Tara's mother said from the top of the steps. "What's going on down there? Is everything all right?"

"Yes, Ma. Kirby's here. He just slipped and fell."

"Is he okay?" Mrs. Copeland started making her way down the long spiral steps.

"Hi, Mrs. Copeland." Kirby turned his face to shield the odor of alcohol fuming from his mouth. "I'm fine, thanks."

"Well, be careful now," Mrs. Copeland admonished after seeing nothing was broken. "Okay, kids, I'm going back to bed."

"Goodnight, Ma."

Kirby and Tara then sat on the couch and quibbled quietly.

"Kirby," Tara said as she rose from the couch, arms flailing in the air, "you have to go on with your life."

"Tara, what're you talkin' about?"

"I'm going to go on with mine. I have no other choice." Tara took a seat again next to Kirby.

"Bennett ..." she said as tears began to well up in her eyes, "he wasn't the first boyfriend I've lost.

My first boyfriend, we were both in the seventh grade. He died of leukemia. We'd been dating for nine months, almost the same amount of time as Bennett and I."

"Tara, I'm sorry. I really am, but—"

"Kirby," Tara rose from her seat once again. This time, with more fury. "No! We have to move on!"

"He was my boy!"

"Well, he was my man!"

After making eye contact, they realized they were at an impasse. In earnest, Tara switched the subject. "I'm getting ready to leave for school soon. Kirby, stay positive. Kathy tells me you've been acting a little strange lately. She says you've been hanging out a lot, and she thinks you've been drinking too much."

"Oh, she does, does she?"

"Well," Tara said a bit more annoyed, "I know you've been drinking. I can smell it on your breath a mile away."

"I don't need this." Kirby lifted himself off the couch and headed for the door.

"Kirby." Tara grabbed him by the arm. "You better get it together. There's a war going on, and all they need is to see you milling around the streets, doing nothing, and they'll draft you, and you'll be over there in Vietnam fighting some senseless war. You'd just have to hope you make it back in one piece."

"Tara," Kirby yanked himself away from her, "you have a good night."

Kirby took to the streets again. He was so intense since he'd left a liquor store for the second time that night, and he'd failed to notice that the heavy downpour had pretty much stopped.

After treading past his building in a trance, he boarded a bus and took a seat in the back. He was alone except for two other passengers seated in the middle. His world was spinning like a top, and for a while, there was no concept of time.

"Whoa! Whoa, bus man," Kirby called out to the driver, now the only other person on the bus. "This is my stop!" He got up slowly and relocated towards the rear door.

"Young man," the salt-and-pepper-haired driver said, "this is a cemetery. This isn't a regular stop at this hour."

Kirby made his way to the front of the bus next to the driver. "Mister, let me off of this bus."

"Young man—"

Kirby began to get agitated, and his facial expression changed. "You better let me off this bus if you know what's good for you."

"Young man, I have a wife and three children at home. I don't want any trouble."

"Good, because you see these," Kirby said. Still slightly inebriated, he displayed his balled fists. "I've already knocked two people out tonight."

"You win." the driver pulled over on the pitch-dark road. "Here's your stop. Have a good evening."

"I thought you might see it my way. Good evening to you, too." Kirby staggered off the bus with a brown bag in tow.

After walking around in circles for several minutes, Kirby reached a second cemetery entrance gate. With very little hesitation, he flung the brown bag package over the fence and into a bushy area.

"Woof! Woof! Woof!" he barked as he looked for another living creature. When there was no response, Kirby looked around.

Then, with the agility of an alley cat, he skillfully scaled the six-foot fence. He recovered his bag with the aid of his flashlight. He then walked and searched tombstone after tombstone.

Finally, he spotted Bennett's, dropped his bag, and sat down in a yoga position. He then tore into the bag open and pulled out a bottle of rum.

"Bennett." He took a swig. "I'm very sorry, man. You shouldn't be layin' there. I should be there." Kirby wiped his face, and in the same motion, threw his head back to accept another quaff. "This is probably all my fault. I mean, you told me about this dream you had about dyin', and I didn't take you seriously. You even told me on several occasions that you thought someone was followin' you, and I didn't listen. Now look at what happened. You get shot right before my very eyes."

Kirby took yet another snootful. "You had so much talent, so much to give, so much to live for. I thought you'd be here forever." He took time to belch, then went back at the rum. "Now look at me. I have no talent, no hope, no desire, no nothin'. You tell me, Bennett ... who should be here, me or you?"

Kirby went into his bag once more, and this time he pulled out a needle and a syringe. But just as he was about to stick himself, a voice from nowhere called out, *"Don't do it. Don't do it to yourself. Kirby, you have so much to live for. You have something to live for. So much to live for ... so much to live for."*

A frightened and troubled Kirby shot back, "Who's there?"

"Don't destroy yourself, Kirby. You have your whole life ahead of you. I love you, Kirby. Don't destroy yourself. Live! Live! Live! Live!"

"Bennett, is that you?"

An unanticipated beam of light jolted Kirby back. A light so intense that he had to squint and shield it with his hands.

"Young man," came a voice from a huge figure in what appeared to be a raincoat. "What're you doing here?" The voice was followed by a growl that belonged to an enormous German shepherd.

"Hey, Mister, hold your dog. Hold your dog!"

"Don't worry about him. You just get outta here before I call the police."

"Go ahead and call them. I could use the free ride home anyway."

"What's in your hand?"

"What? This?" Kirby said, pointing at the bottle. "This is apple juice."

"That's not apple juice."

"It's apple juice."

"That's not apple juice."

"It's apple juice."

"That's not apple juice, young man!" The man yelled, as he tugged his dog. "Matter of fact, I've noticed those bottles around here lately when I do my rounds in the mornings. Have you been sleeping out here?"

"Do I look like a bum to you, Mister? Hey! Call your dog back!"

"Are you gonna leave now, or do I have to call the police."

"I'm goin', Mister, I'm goin'."

The man yanked his dog back again. Fortunately, Kirby wouldn't be his late-night snack.

CHAPTER SEVEN

"It's Wednesday night!" Simon said into the microphone. "Do you guys know what night it is?"

The voices rang from the bleachers of the South Side Mount Vernon Boys & Girls Club. "It's Brotherhood Night!"

The club was located on the corner of Sixth Avenue and Fifth Street. Its gymnasium took up the entire Fifth Street corner block. The outside of the club was coated with bright yellow paint. The basketball court was usually lit with the skylights during the meeting, whereas the normal club lights were of a dim variety. The floor was a caramel marble, and the bleachers accommodated anywhere from fifteen hundred to two thousand bodies.

Simon did a double take when he spotted Kirby standing by the entrance with his two sons.

"You made it," Simon said, approaching them.

The crowd of young men and fathers were singing and clapping to music that was emanating from the public address system.

"Man," Simon said as he hugged Kirby, "I'm awfully glad to see you. I thought you weren't gonna show."

"Kathy and I had to get the boys new sneakers. I told you I'd be here."

"Ah ha, a family outing. See, I told you that you guys will be all right."

"It's not like that. We always get the boys' clothes together."

"Hey, by the way," Simon remembered. "Why'd you hang up on me last night?

"Man, I didn't hang up. I fell asleep. You need to shorten those long and drawn-out jokes of yours."

Simon walked off, laughing. "Well, I saved you a seat on the dais."

Kirby sent his boys to the bleachers and took a seat alongside Boys & Girls Club officials Lowes Moore and James Jones.

The podium was a makeshift chair-and-table ensemble—five chairs and one long table sat in the middle of the gymnasium floor.

Simon, outfitted in a dark blue business suit, white shirt, and paisley tie, made his way back to the mic. He stood in silence for a moment of reflection, as if to absorb the invaluable moment. Simon looked around and noticed the many new faces in the crowd. He then focused on the banners that hung from the rafters. NEW RO IS IN DA HOUSE, YO. TUCKAHOE, ALWAYS ON THE GO. PELHAM, PELHAM, JUST HERE TO TELL HIM.

The presence of black, white, Hispanic, Asian, and many more people of other nationalities intensely moved Simon. The smorgasbord of humanity also netted the likes of gangbangers from rival gangs, would-be gangbangers, drug dealers, drug addicts, pimps, professionals, school kids, and scholars. But the Nation of Islam provided security, so there was no need to feel uncomfortable.

Simon detested the fact that people had to be governed but rationalized that it was for the best.

Kirby, for one, was somewhat taken aback by the masses that ranged from eight-year-olds to senior citizens. The crowd spilled out onto the floor and up and down both baselines.

At the start of Simon's lectures, he'd always request for all those seated in groups to disperse. He wanted everyone to sit next to someone foreign to themselves. He encouraged peace among diversity and took pride in his ability to say the word *peace* in several different languages.

Simon's mind went adrift to when he was in prison. One night, while alone in his cell, lying face down in a deep sleep, Simon felt a poke to his back.

"Wake up! Wake up, I said, Simon!"

Simon thought it was a guard doing a routine bed check and offered sheepishly, "What is it? What do you want? Go bother somebody else and leave me alone."

"Wake up, Simon!" The voice and poke came again. Only this time, the voice was louder and the poke much harder.

"Man, it's early. I'm going back to sleep. Good night."

"Wake up, Simon! Now!" the voice ordered yet again. This time, with even more force than before.

Simon still elected to ignore the orders. That was until he felt a smack to his back that felt as if it'd come from a baseball bat. Simon turned over hastily and was blinded by a bright light. His fears became even more intense when he realized the light wasn't from a prison guard's flashlight. The light that appeared before him seemed to come from a doorway nine feet tall and three feet wide.

"What's going on?" Simon asked with fear and trembling. "Are you here to kill me?"

"Simon!" the voice cried out. "You have blood on your hands!"

Cowering, Simon tried to duck beneath the cover of blankets. A gust of freezing wind whisked through the cell and sliced through him.

"I'm sorry! I'm so sorry for what I've done!"

"You have a debt to pay, Simon."

"I'll do anything! Anything! Please, don't kill me! I'll do whatever you ask!"

"Save the lives you've ruined. Save the lives you've ruined! You have blood on your hands!"

"How do I do that?" Simon said, still trembling as he heard babies crying. The voices then stopped and gave way to the sound of gunshots.

"You owe, Simon! You owe!"

******

Within minutes, the musical chairs had stopped, and everyone was settled again. This time, when Simon approached the mic, the ovation was louder and stronger.

"Please take the hand of your neighbor. Then let's bow our heads in a moment of silence out of respect for those who've fallen needlessly to gang violence." As Simon bowed his head, he hoped others would pray in silence as he did. "Peace to all of you."

"Peace to you to, Bruh Simon," the mass of humanity roared back.

"Thank you, and it's so good to see you all. I won't be long. I don't care to trouble your patience."

"Take your time, Bruh Simon! This is your night!" a voice came from the audience.

"No, no. We have school children here, and I want to be mindful. Anyway, I'm gonna get right to it. I'm appealing to you young men and some of you young women." Simon stopped for a moment and smiled. "Yeah, I see you've infiltrated the ranks. It's okay for now. You're most welcome. But on a serious note, we must stop the killing. You gangbangers, pushers, dealers, stop the madness. These guns … hey, if you guys want to shoot something, shoot basketballs, not bullets! Some of you guys have been doing a good job, a great job with the Midnight Hoops here at the club. You must continue it. Shoot hoops, not guns. Not drugs!

"You guys doing these drugs, you guys are killing yourselves, your communities, and your families. Fella, look at the big picture. Really, what good is it to gain the whole world and lose your soul and kill off a brother or sister in the process?

It really isn't worth it. And yes, I'm speaking from experience. I've been there. I was a menace to society just like some of you.

I sold dope. I hooked women, and I ran numbers. But it took me going to prison for the light to get turned on again. And I said again because you're looking at a man with a master's degree in psychology."

Simon saw murmuring throughout the crowd. "Yes, I said a master's degree. I lost my way for a time, but through the help of God and my lovely wife, I was able to come back. Some of you, if you dared to go that way, or for those of you in it, may not make it back. If you will, please come back while you have the chance. You may not get the same privilege as I did. You might die before you're able to turn your life around.

"I can't tell you guys how to serve God. That's your natural right under the United States Constitution. But by and large, educate yourselves! Read books! Learn more about life. You guys that are in school, stay there until the duration. Complete the necessary requirements in order to get that piece of paper. Fellas, education is the key that unlocks the door to so many opportunities. Take full advantage of that.

"I want you people to know something. I had the opportunity to earn thousands of dollars on the lecture circuit, but I forfeited that opportunity. Why? Because I love you fellas. And I want to see each and every one of you make it. I don't want to see you fellas, especially those of you at risk, to go out like that. I want to see you go far in this life and be the men you can become. I want to see you fellas living in peace with one another. Yes, black, white, Hispanic, Asian, Indian, Native, Jew or Gentile, rich man or poor man. Let's all live here in peace and harmony."

Simon stepped away from the podium and received a thunderous round of applause. "And one more thing I want to add in my closing remarks. I want you guys to stand. No, not physically stand, but spiritually stand! Make a stand! Take a stand!

And stand for something right!

Something positive! Something true! Because if you don't, you'll fall for anything!"

Simon concluded by raising his hand in a peace gesture as the crowd rose again and showered him with cheers, whistles, and a thunderous round of applause.

As always, Simon asked, "You guys ready for this one?"

"Yeah!" came the jubilant response.

"Okay, here goes. Agnes, a local socialite was having this gathering, a tea party of sorts for the ladies' cultural club. Agnes spent days on end preparing for this gala event. And all was going well, that is, until little Abner, her four-year-old son, came running in and yelling, 'Mummie! Mummie! Mummie! I think I gotta make a pee-pee.'

"Embarrassed and humiliated, Agnes ushered little Abner upstairs and gave him a tongue lashing. 'Son, the next time you have to make a pee-pee, don't yell. Just come to me and tell me. You have to whisper.'

"Little Abner took the scolding to heart and went back out to play.

"That night, after everyone was asleep, little Abner awoke and went into his parents' bedroom. He started jumping up and down and tugged on his daddy's nightshirt. Reluctantly, his daddy woke up. 'What do you want, little Abner?' big Abner said.

"'I gotta whisper, Daddy. I need to whisper really bad.'

"'Whisper? Surely, son.' Big Abner leaned his head over the side of the bed. 'Just whisper right in my ear.'"

The seriousness of the gathering suddenly changed to mass hysteria. Simon found himself in stitches as he laughed all the way back to his office.

"Bruh Simon, can I speak to you a minute?"

"Sure, Rickey, come on in. Have a seat."

Rickey Gates was one of the fellas from the neighborhood. Rickey, twenty-four years old, was part of a large family that consisted of six brothers and seven sisters. His family had a strange genetic trait—they all had lazy left eyes.

"What can I do for you?"

"Yeah, Bruh Simon. I want to tell you, your speech really moved me. I mean really, really moved me. I mean really ..."

"Thank you, Rickey. Now what's up."

"Oh, yeah, yeah ... well, as I was sitting there listened to you speak—"

"*Listened* to me speak?"

"Sorry, I meant, listening to you speak. I was saying to myself, what can I do to contribute to this situation. You know, help out some."

"Of course."

"Well, here goes. I started to write this poem. You see, alittle somethin' to represent the sistas."

"You have it there? Let's hear it."

"Check it out, check it out, check it out."

"I'm checking, I'm checking, I'm checking already."

"Here's the title: *Da Freaks Wit Da Big Onions*."

Simon crossed his eyes and slid back in his chair. "Whoa! Whoa! Whoa! What!"

"*Da Freaks Wit Da Big Onions*. You know, it's about those girlies with they ... pow, pow!"

"Rickey." Simon pointed toward the door. "Get outta my office! Get out now! If you wanna stay for midnight basketball, feel free, but in the meantime, get out. Read a book or something. Go to one of the reading workshops, but don't take that with you. Please don't."

"Aw, Bruh Simon, this is just my creative genius. My way of sayin'—"

"Bye, Rickey."

"I'm out. Oh, hey, Kirby, how you doin'?"

"I'm cool," Kirby said and held the door for the departing poet. "Simon, was that Rickey Gates?"

"Yeah, that's him." Simon shook his head in disbelief.

"His mind is bad, ain't it?"

"Yeah, but I think something's wrong with the whole family. If you ask me, I think somewhere down the line, some of his relatives married each other."

Kirby closed the door and took the seat Rickey had just occupied. "They can't be that bad."

"Da freaks wit da big onions."

"What did you say? Simon, you still tryna tell those corny jokes?"

"What corny jokes, chump? Where's your sense of humor?"

"Humor? Where's my sense of humor? Where's your sense of dignity? Chump."

Simon leaped from his chair and hopped across his desk, knocking over a paper bin in the process. "Chump?" Simon fixed himself into a boxing stance. "I'll show you *chump*. Put 'em up."

Kirby lifted himself out of his seat and joined Simon in the imaginary ring.

"Talk is cheap, you know."

"Oh, so I suppose listening to you is expensive?"

"Old man, you don't want none of this."

"Old?" Simon took a jab at the air and missed by a country mile. "I'll show you old. I ain't lost nothing."

"Of course," Kirby said and returned an errant jab. "How can you lose something you never had? Ever."

Right at that moment, the office door swung open just before the *old Golden Gloves* were about to hurt themselves—pull a muscle, strain a ligament, or break a bone.

"Is this a private affair, or can anyone join?" Jimmy Jones, Director of the South Side Boys & Girls Club, said upon entering. Mr. Jones and Regional Director, Billy Thomas were the masterminds behind getting Simon to join the staff. They also gave him the idea, citing his personality and gift of gab, of having Brotherhood Night and the Midnight Basketball Tournament.

"Hey, Jim," Kirby said as the two shook hands. "What time is it?"

"10:30."

"Whoa, Kathy's gonna kill me. I better get the boys home. It's past their bedtime. I'll see you fellas later."

"Those boys are growing up fast. They're a good size. I could definitely use them on the Junior Sonics. Bring them by on Saturday at 3:30, if you can."

"Sounds good, but if I can't make it, I'll have Kathy bring them by. They'll play either way."

Jim was dressed in a brown three-piece suit. "Good. Tell Kathy I said hello ..." he said to a pooped-out Kirby, "and Simon, don't forget our board meeting on Friday at 1:00."

"I'll be there, boss. Oh!"

"Something wrong?"

"Oh, no, it's just, I promised my daughter I'd take her to her ballet lesson on Friday. But—"

"What time is her lesson?"

"4:30."

"We should be long finished by then, but if not, then just leave. It's just a briefing. Don't want you to break any promises."

At the end, Simon had a moment to reflect on the day's events. He thought of his speech and felt a chill. The response he'd received was the greatest ever, and that included all the sermons he'd preached in church.

It was an hour and a half before Midnight Basketball, so Simon decided to change into his warm-up gear. As he reached out to lock the door, he felt a strange tug coming from the other side. Thinking it was jammed, he tugged away at it again. This time, with more force. It opened, and who did he see—Jay Rock, all six-feet-five inches of him. Jay Rock, who weighed 250 pounds, sported a toothpick, and had two front teeth studded in diamonds.

"Can I help you?" Simon asked in surprise and shock at the massive man standing before him.

"Yeah, you can." Jay Rock bogarted his way in. Once he was in, he flicked his toothpick onto the floor and motioned for Simon to sit down.

"Look here, Jay Rock," Simon said as he noticed Jay Rock open his vest and flash his six-inch knife. "I'm drenched. I was just about to change my clothes. I'll—"

"This'll only take a few minutes. Have a seat ... please?" Jay Rock's voice seemed to take on a different tone. A much deeper and more deliberate one.

Simon unwillingly yielded to Jay Rock's request. "Okay, I'm sitting. What can I do for you?"

"Well," Jay Rock started and dropped his size fourteens atop Simon's desk, "I gotta give it to you. You definitely have a way of captivating people. I mean, the way you can get their attention and keep it for a long period of time, that's a gift."

"Thank you," Simon said and reached across the desk to slap down the combined twenty-eight inches.

"I truly appreciate your speeches, like I said. But the reality is, you takin' away from my business. You takin' food off my table, and I don't like that."

"Say what?"

"You got customers leavin' me and convertin' to what you're tellin' them. Some of my workers have also gone soft on me."

Simon sat back and felt his oats. The idea of his pearls of wisdom reaching a few made him even more confident. "I'm sorry, but I can't help you," he shot back with a coy smile.

Jay Rock again opened his vest. This time, a tad bit wider. "Man, listen. And get that sappy smile off your face. This is serious business."

"Jay Rock, your Boy Scout knife don't scare me one bit. Your size don't scare me either. Man, I ate guys like you up for breakfast in the joint."

"This is Mount Vernon. This ain't no cell block, and I ain't one of your little cellmates."

"You don't care about what you're doing to your own people, do you? Some people in society just love it when we kill each other. You're feeding right into their hands."

"Yo, Simon, you were just like me once. And now you're so righteous. Holier than thou. You ain't no better than me. I'm survivin'. I'm gettin' mines. And I'll die for mines, to protect mines. That's my word."

"There's always a better way of surviving. Get a job. A real job. Get out there and hustle like everybody else. And the fact that you're willing to die or be killed rather like a dog in the streets ... I don't get it. Do you realize there are a number of merchants in this area alone who are scared to death when school lets out at 3:00? In fact, some even go so far as to close their stores at that time. They're scared of the children, and what kind of example do you think you're setting? Does it make sense to you at all?"

"Whether it makes sense to me or not, it's not my problem, and it ain't my concern. I have my own business to run." Jay Rock flashed his knife again. "The merchants or whoever gotta do what they gotta do. I ain't scared of nothin'."

The repellent conversation continued for nearly an hour, until Simon's patience ran out.

"Jay Rock, this conversation is over!"

He gave Simon a dirty look, sucking his teeth. "Man, you better watch yourself and stay out of my business."

"Just get out," Simon said, opening the door. Just as it opened, his wife appeared.

"Honey, what's up? Whoa, stop!" TyDixie had to step in front of Simon to keep him from going after Jay Rock.

"Stay away from my kids, Jay Rock! Stay away from my kids!"

******

"Kathy," Kirby said as he sat on his couch and popped a pill, "I have the boys with me. You weren't home, and I didn't want to leave them alone. I'll run them off to school tomorrow. I understand you went to the mall with your mother. That's fine, but it was getting late, and my head started hurting. Yes, I'm getting it checked out first chance I get. Woman, please, will you stop questioning me! You're stressin' me! Kathy? Kathy? Hello ... this woman hung up on me. Well, I'll be—"

"Daddy," Bennie said, walking into the living room, "who you talkin' to? Mommy?"

Bennie was described by many to be as cute as a button. But he didn't favor Kirby or Kathy, with his huge dimples that sheltered each cheek and curly, dark brown hair.

"No, son," Kirby said, holding his head. "Is your brother out of the bathroom?"

"Yes."

"Well, you guys get in bed, and I'll be there in a minute to tuck y'all in."

"Okay, Daddy. When are you comin' back home?"

"Uh, I don't know right now."

"I ... I mean, we miss you bein' there with us."

"I miss being with you guys also."

"Daddy, you all right?"

"I'm fine, Bennie. Now go on, get in the bed."

"Why you holdin' your head like that then?"

Kirby lifted his head momentarily to answer. "No reason, son. Now go on." He tapped the backside of the interrogator in the red and blue Superman pajamas.

CHAPTER EIGHT

JULY 1973

The sun glistened as brightly as ever on this midsummer's day. Two weeks had passed since Bennett was buried. But that was hardly adequate time for Kirby to get over anything. Especially since he was so dissatisfied with the way the police had been handling or mishandling the situation.

He felt the police were way off-base in the way they'd gone about their investigation. He nearly came to blows with one detective after his mother was asked to go the police station for questioning.

As the days whisked away, his ever-growing disdain for the city he called home mounted. Reading the local papers and watching the local news became increasingly depressing.

Kirby decided he wanted to shoot some hoops at the Fourth Street playground. A first since he and Bennett played there several months ago. He knew the event would be difficult and refused to go through it alone. So he called Dexter and Big Joe and asked them to hang. They agreed on the condition that Kirby would promise to lighten up and allow himself to enjoy the moment. Kirby agreed but crossed his fingers during the pledge.

Following several games of Horse, Out, Twenty-One, and after working on drills, the three amigos decided to listen to the message their bodies were sending—*take a rest*. Surprisingly, Kirby sprang for soft drinks and purchased them from the hot dog truck stationed just outside the park.

"Thanks, Kirby, that hit the spot," Dexter said as he lay sun-soaked, sprawled across the wooden bleachers.

Big Joe, who was on his second sixteen-ounce Pepsi, managed to toast the air and nod his approval.

"Don't mention it. Besides, I owed you for takin' my spot on the Sonics."

"No problem," Dexter said as beads of sweat emitted from skin. "I needed the practice time anyway."

"S-s-so d-d-did you m-m-make up your mind about w-w-what you gonna do?"

"Not quite, big fella. I have somethin' in mind though."

Dexter had had enough of being cooked by the sun and decided to sit up. "You're not gonna stay around here and do nothing, are you?"

"B-b-but y-y-you," in frustration, Big Joe stomped the ground and pounded on the basketball, "ain't gonna try t-t-to be no detective, are you?"

Kirby held up his hands. "I plead the fifth."

"Let the police handle this, man," Dexter offered.

"The police? Who, Mutt and Jeff?"

"Kirby, I know you may've been closer to Bennett than we were, but we love him just the same. He was our boy, too. I don't want you gettin' yourself hurt or killed, dude."

"Yeah, but do you think Bennett is restin' comfortably in his grave? He's probably turnin' over as we speak, knowin' the person who killed him is still on the loose."

"Kirby—"

"Forget it, Dex." Kirby waved his hand. "When are you guys leavin' for school?"

"I sh-sh-ship out Au-Au-August 22nd."

"I don't know yet," Dexter said, visibly still annoyed. "A teammate of mine is supposed to call me to let me know when the apartment will be ready. But my guess would be mid to late August like Big Joe."

"Well, I hope you both make it to the NBA. I could sure use those free tickets to Knicks games. Either that or sell them for some moolah."

"I knew there was a catch to those sodas," Dexter said to Big Joe, and the two slapped five.

"Very funny." Kirby playfully shoved Dexter. He then glanced over his shoulder as two of his favorite little people entered the park. "Yvette and Dannon!"

Dannon located the voice and ran towards Kirby as fast as his little legs would carry him.

"Kirby!" Dannon jumped into his arms.

Kirby proudly held him tight and kissed him on the back of his head. "How you doin', little man?" Kirby then bent over to kiss Yvette on her forehead.

"Hey, Kirby!" Yvette shot back with excitement.

"Where you guys comin' from?"

"Aunt Traci's house," Dannon answered as Kirby let him down.

"Is it hot enough for you guys?" Kirby asked as the perspiration drowned his body.

"It's too hot. I'm gettin' ready to go back inside." Yvette wiped her forehead with the back of her hand.

"How's your mother? Give her my regards."

"Okay, we will. See you later."

As Kirby made his way back to his buddies on the bleachers, he peered outside the park and saw a female with a very shapely body wearing a pink tank top and matching shorts.

Big Joe noticed Kirby's trance and followed the path of his eyes. "V-v-very n-n-nice. I-I-I'd l-l-love to walk her home."

"That's Angela!" Dexter said.

"Angela?" Kirby said and sprinted off toward her.

Dexter and Big Joe unsuccessfully tried to restrain him.

Kirby reached Angela within a twinkling of an eye, and she immediately protested his existence.

"Angela, wait."

"Why did you mention my name to the police, Kirby? I'm a potential suspect now. I can't believe you."

"Look, Angela ..." Kirby tried to reason.

"Kirby, you weasel. I loved Bennett. Why would I want to kill him? That doesn't make any sense."

Kirby's gentle yank of Angela's arm was enough to get her to stop and give him an ear.

"I'm sorry, Angela, but when the cops asked me for names of those I thought had problems with Bennett, I remembered you. The day in the hall when you threatened him over the deal that happened with you and Mr. Whitby."

"Kirby, that was nothing. I was only angry for a second, no matter what the deal was. I was only angry for a short time."

"I had to do what I thought was best. I told the truth. I mean, like where were you anyway when everything happened?"

"What!" Angela answered in surprise and shock. "Check the photo in the newspaper the day it happened. I was standing right in front of the podium, listening to his speech just like everyone else. What, are you crazy or something?"

"Well, I was asked questions, so I answered them. That was my man."

"Kirby, I was embarrassed, but I was also very scared, getting yelled at like that by the police."

"Angela."

"They had a bright light shining in my face and a tape recorder. It was a mess. I had to get a lawyer, and my mother was a basket case."

"Hey, I'm sorry but—"

"Oh, yeah, and as far as Mr. Whitby is concerned, he was questioned, too."

"He was?"

"Of course, he was, but he had an alibi. He was out of town, attending his nephew's wedding in Philly."

"But—"

"Listen, Kirby," Angela said in a tone that expressed intolerance for Kirby's public, informal interrogation. "Let the police handle this. Let *them* handle it. Goodbye!"

Kirby gazed back at the park, but his boys were nowhere to be found. Instead of retreating home to escape the bristling sun, he chose to head to the Mount Vernon police station.

CHAPTER NINE

The hike to the police station was exhausting and left Kirby sweaty and dehydrated. The red-brick station house was located downtown, adjacent to City Hall—the place where Bennett was fatally wounded.

Inside, the station had the look of an old-time jailhouse, with paint-chipped walls, outdated rotary dial telephones, rusted gray metal desks, and graffiti-smeared cells that housed ten to twelve prisoners at a time.

Kirby made his way over to a white-haired police officer who was wasting time with a cup of coffee and a glazed donut. "Officer Pickman?" Kirby said after reading the stubby fellow's badge.

"Yes, young man, what can I do for you?"

"Well, you can start off by tellin' me if you've made any arrests yet."

"Arrests?"

"Yeah," Kirby said, this time with more volume, which caused others to look at him. "Do you have any arrests in the Bennett Wilson murder?"

The answer Kirby received wasn't the one he wanted. But he figured as much. In a fit of rage, he stormed out of the station, mumbling unpleasantries under his breath.

"Kirby!" Detective Bill Baines said, catching Kirby before he could cross the street.

Baines was formerly one of Mount Vernon's two truant officers. He stood six-feet tall and had a bald head and dark complexion. He flexed his twenty-three-inch biceps, awaiting Kirby's response.

"I don't have anything to say."

Baines stopped in his tracks and looked at Kirby as he continued to walk away. "Kirby, talk to me. Now!"

"Mr. Baines—"

"Hey, listen. We're doing all we can under the circumstances."

"Circumstances! Please spare me."

"Now hold it right there. I've known you both a long time. I know your families. You know that if I had any information, anything at all, you'd know about it. But right now, there are no suspects."

"No suspects!"

"None. Every name you gave us, every person we've checked out was clean. They all had an airtight alibi. Either they were there at the scene, or they were out of town. Either way, Kirby, they're no longer considered suspects. I know he wasn't into any organized crime or anything, but his death, especially the way it was done, is very strange. Very, very strange. But we're still working on it. You can rest assured."

Kirby felt that the police had let him down, Mr. Baines included, and had no more interest in continuing the discussion. He reluctantly shook Mr. Baines's hand and went about his way.

******

Close to 11:00 that night, after drowning his sorrows, Kirby roamed the streets. Aimlessly, he drifted and drifted, chasing Pink Elephants until he reached the Yonkers city limits. The South Yonkers city limits to be exact. He remembered that Shorty lived there and usually hung out at Slappy's pool hall, so he staggered along, hoping to run into him so that he could make him talk.

He reached Slappy's pool hall and was greeted by a cloud of cigarette and cheap cigar smoke, the sound of the Temptations blasting from the jukebox, and the knocking of pool balls.

Kirby saw Slappy standing behind the counter, giving change, and selling drinks.

He was a middle-aged man around fifty years old, short, semi-bald, and he wore a plain, white t-shirt and brown vest as his everyday uniform. His nickname stuck and became the name of his business. *Slappy*, was a play on 'knee-slapper.' Slappy, in his younger days, was a stand-up comedian, as well as a bartender.

"Slappy, let me have one of those, please."

"Kirby, my man," Slappy said. "Let me see some ID."

"Come on Slap, you know I'm legal."

"I almost forgot. I hadn't seen you in a while. What brings you this way?"

Now taking a swig before answering, Kirby had to cover his mouth to muffle a burp that needed to escape. He replied, "I have some business to tend to."

"Business?" Slappy now asked. "What kind of business?" They both turned to the sudden cluster of noise.

Shorty Stokes and his mob had burst through the doorway. As they entered, the crowd went quiet.

Looking at Shorty, Kirby slammed down his empty glass, and said, "That's my business." He then jumped up and made his way toward the mob.

"Kirby!"

******

Close to 11:00 that night, after drowning his sorrows, Kirby roamed the streets. Aimlessly, he drifted and drifted, chasing Pink Elephants until he reached the Yonkers city limits. The South Yonkers city limits to be exact. He remembered that Shorty lived there and usually hung out at Slappy's pool hall, so he staggered along, hoping to run into him so that he could make him talk.

He reached Slappy's pool hall and was greeted by a cloud of cigarette and cheap cigar smoke, the sound of the Temptations blasting from the jukebox, and the knocking of pool balls.

Kirby saw Slappy standing behind the counter, giving change, and selling drinks. He was a middle-aged man around fifty years old, short, semi-bald, and he wore a white t-shirt and brown vest as his everyday outfit. His nickname stuck and became the name of his business. *Slappy*, was a play on 'knee-slapper.' Slappy, in his younger days, was a stand-up comedian, as well as a bartender.

"Slappy, let me have one of those, please."

"Kirby, my man," Slappy said. "Let me see some ID."

"Come on Slap, you know I'm legal."

"I almost forgot. I hadn't seen you in a while. What brings you this way?"

Now taking a swig before answering, Kirby had to cover his mouth to muffle a burp that needed to escape. He replied, "I have some business to tend to."

"Business?" Slappy now asked. "What kind of business?" They both turned to the sudden cluster of noise.

Shorty Stokes and his mob had burst through the doorway. As they entered, the crowd went quiet.

Looking at Shorty, Kirby slammed down his empty glass, and said, "That's my business." He then jumped up and made his way toward the mob.

"Kirby!"

As drunk as he was, Kirby still remembered the quintet, particularly the tallest one with the chrome dome and scar on his forehead. Some time ago, he and Bennett beat them senseless. The one who had the bushy afro looked as though he'd never recovered from the broken nose he'd suffered at Bennett's hands.

He noticed Shorty's two front teeth were still missing. Bennett had cracked him good. The other two were sporting dark shades in the dead of night.

"Shorty! What's up!"

Shorty looked at Kirby and scowled, cracking his knuckles. "I've been waitin' for this moment a long time." He then sucker-punched Kirby straight in the gut.

Kirby gasped. As he grimaced in pain, all doubled over, twenty or so patrons scattered like roaches throughout the dim room.

Two of the men, one wearing shades and the bald one, snatched Kirby from behind. While they held Kirby, Shorty pounded away at Kirby's face. Blood spurted from Kirby's nose and mouth. His consciousness began slipping away. Shorty now took the opportunity to grab the nearest pool stick and whack the crown of Kirby's head, sending shockwaves to the balls of his feet. Intense pain at the base of Kirby's skull made the room violently spin.

"That's enough!" Slappy yelled. "Stop! Before I call the police!"

Shorty pointed to him. "Shut your mouth before you get some, too!"

One of the hoods grabbed the now slumped-over Kirby and threw him headfirst into a wood-paneled wall. The hoodlums all laughed hysterically and made their way over.

Shorty retrieved a .22-caliber pistol from inside his jacket, asking, "You ready to go home now, chump?"

"No," Kirby faintly answered.

Shorty laughed, removing bullets. "You wanna meet your maker?"

"I don't wanna die," Kirby said through a stream of tears. "Please don't kill me."

"Aw, he's begging," Shorty said. "You know how to play Russian Roulette?"

Fear jolted through Kirby's body and had paralyzed him. Shorty leaned in, spun the chamber of the handgun, placed it against Kirby's temple, and whispered in his ear, "If I pull this trigger, maybe you won't die. But if I shoot you ... bye-bye."

He squeezed. The first click, an empty chamber, caused Kirby's body to shudder in panic, attempting to jerk himself free from the heavy-handed grip. Shorty then rose to his feet, cackling again with his friends as they watched Kirby squirm.

"Please don't kill me." Squinting to regain focus, Kirby begged, "Don't shoot me. I don't wanna die."

"Shut up, you sissy! You should've thought about that before you came lookin' for me all incorrect."

Shorty unmercifully squeezed the trigger. Once more, Kirby flinched and panicked. This time, relieving his bladder and saturating his pants.

"Enough!" Simon shouted as he, Big Willie, and Little Tiny Smalls entered the pool hall.

"Get 'um!" Shorty motioned with his head. First to his henchmen and then to their intended target.

"I need this exercise," Willie said as he uncorked a punch that pummeled the hood with the scar on his face.

The force of that blow made the guy's whole body stiffen before he fell. One of the shady characters let out a loud roar, picked up a pool stick, and charged after Little Tiny. Little Tiny, undaunted, jumped into a fencing position with his walking cane. That is until he grew tired of the shenanigans and dropped the guy with a blow to the head.

Willie ran over to the other shaded punk, who was frightened out of his wits. Willie elected not to use his hands. He head-butted him instead.

The last one, the one sporting the afro, foolishly hopped on Little Tiny's back and began beating him upside the head. Little Tiny remained calm. There was no need to worry. He simply let go of his cane, grabbed the man by the hands, and flipped him over.

For some asinine reason only known to him, the guy wouldn't quit. He leaped off his back and lunged toward Little Tiny. Little Tiny picked up his cane, broke into a batting stance reminiscent of Hank Aaron waiting for a fastball, and whacked him on the noggin.

Shorty saw the destruction of his men and felt helpless. He pulled his piece on Simon and said, "I'll take you outta here right now!"

"Young boy, you ain't got the guts. And you certainly don't have the hardware," Simon said as he, Big Willie, and Little Tiny Smalls showed off their pieces.

Shorty felt defeated and sucked his snaggy teeth.

"Get that toy from him, Willie." Simon walked over to Kirby.

Willie snatched the gun away from Shorty, looked at it, frowned, and pimp-slapped him. The smack was real—hard and loud. Shorty would've done the United States gymnastics team very proud. He did a pirouette, a somersault, and a dismount over not one, but two pool tables. Thus, another tooth was lost.

Willie laughed and yelled, "9.5!" Then he gave Simon a five and handed him the gun.

"Thanks, Willie." Simon accepted it. "Do me a favor. You and Tiny take this trash outta here. I'll see how little man is doin'."

Slappy suddenly reappeared from behind the counter and asked, "Is it over yet?"

Simon looked at him and furiously clamored, "You were back there all this time and let this happen?"

"I-I-I-I ..."

"You could've at least called the police!"

"I-I-I-I ..."

"Forget him, Simon." Willie waved his hand at Slappy. "You know he ain't nothing but a washerwoman anyway."

Simon returned his attention to a half-dazed Kirby. He reached into his jacket pocket and pulled out a white handkerchief. Kirby resisted but then accepted at Simon's persistence. Kirby was perplexed. More from Simon's assistance than the battering he'd taken.

"Fear not, man. I'm not gonna hurt you."

Kirby shoved the bloodied handkerchief in front of Simon's face.

"No, you can keep it." Simon smiled. "I know you're probably wondering what I'm doing here."

"The thought did cross my mind."

"The answer is, I like you, kid. I think you have a lotta guts. But as you just saw, guts could've got you killed."

"I was just tryin' to find out who killed Bennett. No one is givin' me answers. Why am I tellin' you this anyway." Kirby grimaced and grabbed his right side.

"Your ribs are probably broken."

"No kiddin', Sherlock."

Simon felt slightly insulted by Kirby's remark but managed a smile. "That's okay. I can take it. But you have to let the police handle this. Didn't the cop tell you so earlier today?"

Kirby looked Simon in his eyes, and that confirmed what he was thinking.

"Yeah, I was following you. I've been keeping an eye out. I wanted you protected. I figured you might run into something like this sooner or later. It was just a matter of time."

Gratitude got the best of Kirby as he managed a smile through his swollen, crimson lips. "What took you so long then?"

"You want to know the truth. Well ... Willie had to get something to eat. Don't laugh, you're gonna hurt yourself. Listen, I know you may not want to hear this, but you need to let the police handle this investigation. This thing is bigger than you. In my opinion, Bennett's murder has all the makings of a hit. I know he wasn't into anything heavy, but it sure smells like one. The cops won't tell you that."

"How do you figure?"

"It was done from long range. Almost as if it was done from another part of the city, and the gun used was a high-powered one. Nothing like this toy thing here." Simon looked at the gun he still had in his possession. "Besides ... Shorty and his guys are chumps. Look, see, no bullets. He tried that Russian Roulette garbage on you just to scare you. He wasn't gonna shoot you."

"Well," Kirby looked down at his damp pants leg, "he certainly had me fooled."

"Let's get outta here. Lemme take you home. Or do you want me to take you to the hospital?"

"No hospital." Kirby attempted to get to his feet, with little success. "I can make it."

"Yeah, right. I'm taking you home." Simon helped Kirby to his feet.

Kirby left the pool hall, hanging onto Simon's shoulder.

CHAPTER TEN

"Son, my God, what happened to you?" a frightened Lois asked as she caught Kirby in her arms.

"Momma, I had a little trouble that's all."

"Trouble? What kind of trouble? You look like you're hurt. I'm calling the police."

"No, Momma. No, it's been taken care of already."

Ms. Maxwell sat her devastated and wounded son down on the couch before going to the kitchen. She pulled out a box of Arm & Hammer baking soda and a plastic yellow pail from the closet and filled it with warm water.

Kirby begged his mother not to call the police or the ambulance as she patted his bruises, trying to soothe and ease the pain.

She eventually dropped the idea of calling for help, but not until after Kirby explained what was going on. Her son's predicament would no longer be a mystery. She wanted and demanded answers.

Ms. Maxwell sternly implored him to end his alcohol abuse. "Kirby, you have to stop this drinking. Please stop it. Son, if you have problems, I don't care what they are, come and talk to me about them. I know you're a man and you have your own personal things going, but son, I'm your mother, and I love you with all my heart. I'll listen to you even if I don't understand you. I'm here for you."

"I know, Momma, I—"

"And if I weren't here, if God decided to take my life, I know someone else will emerge in your life for you to talk to. Please, please stop drinking. And for God's sake, please don't start doin' no drugs."

Kirby, at last, came clean with his mother and told her everything he'd been going through since his best friend's death.

He gave her details of the events leading up to and including when he was beaten to a pulp by Shorty and his boys. Kirby also confessed that he was rescued by a person that he'd wished would die a vicious death.

"Kirby, you have to stop snooping around for answers about Bennett."

"Yes, Momma, I—"

"Son," Mrs. Maxwell grabbed Kirby by his shoulders, "I don't want to lose you. Especially due to you getting yourself killed." She turned her head toward the living room window. "Every night, I can hear Betty crying," Mrs. Maxwell continued, talking more to herself than to Kirby as she stared into the abyss of the night.

Kirby gave his mother a blank and confused look.

"No, son. Not literally. I mean, I can hear her soul crying out to her son. Bennett was her child, her firstborn. Kirby, I don't want to lose you that way. So please keep yourself outta trouble and let the police handle it. We all hurt, but realistically, what can we do?"

"Momma, I miss him. I miss Bennett. Every time the telephone rings or there's a knock on the door, I just hope and wish it could be him, sayin', *Kirb, it was all a joke. Let's go play ball or get something to eat.* But then I go to his gravesite and see his name engraved on that tombstone." Kirby laid his head in his mother's lap. "Momma! Why did somebody have to kill him? He never hurt nobody. And why can't they find out who did it? Why, Momma? Why?"

Kirby and his mother rapped until the early hours of the morning. He shared his immediate and future intentions. Kirby mentioned that he was considering joining the Navy, and she vehemently opposed it. She cited the ongoing Vietnam War as her primary cause for concern. Kirby said that he knew of the risks and assured her as best he could that he probably wouldn't see any action.

"Momma," Kirby said as reassuringly as possible, "I believe in myself, and I think I'll be all right."

"Son, I believe in you, too, but war is what it is ... war."

"I don't wanna die, but I remember a conversation I had with Bennett. I told him when I die, I wanna die with some dignity and not like some animal in the streets or strung out on drugs."

"Son, I'm so scared of losing you, but on the other hand, I'm so proud of you. You're a man now. You've grown up right before my very eyes." Ms. Maxwell kissed Kirby's forehead.

"Now, Momma," Kirby said playfully, "don't get all mushy and stuff."

"I'm so proud of you."

"Momma ..."

"Have you told Kathy yet?"

Kirby sighed. "No, I haven't. You're the first person I've mentioned this to."

Mrs. Maxwell stared into Kirby's eyes. "You really love Kathy, don't you?"

"Yeah, Momma, I do."

"How do you think her parents will feel about it?"

"Well, her father was in the Navy," Kirby said with a sly smile. "That's my ace in the hole."

"You are so crazy," Ms. Maxwell said, giving Kirby a playful tap on the arm. "Just be yourself." She then reverted to the previous subject. "I trust you've checked long and hard on the Navy thing? When would you ship out? What's going on?"

"Momma," Kirby said, grim-faced, "I think I'd be shippin' out in a month or so. I think I need to get outta here as soon as possible."

"So how do you propose to marry any time soon, or are you?"

"I'm figuring six to seven months. I could marry her during a break."

"Kirby," Mrs. Maxwell deadpanned, "please tell me Kathy isn't pregnant."

"Yeah, Momma ..."

"Yeah?"

"No, I mean, no. She's not pregnant."

"Thank you, son, thank you. Get yourselves together first, then have children. Anyway, let me go finish cooking."

******

Two weeks had flown by, and Kirby was still bedridden and mending his wounds. Kathy's parents had already given the okay on his marriage proposal, so his mood was better. He was viewing his favorite TV show when his mother yelled to him that he had visitors.

"Hey, Buddy," Dexter said as he and Big Joe entered. He sat on the edge of Kirby's bed, while Big Joe grabbed a fold-up chair from the hallway. "How're you feelin' today?"

"I'm all right. I think I'm startin' to feel normal again. Thanks for askin'. How're you guys doin'?"

"B-b-better th-th-than y-y-you are of-of-of co-co-course."

"O-o-of co-co-course," Kirby chimed in.

"Now you guys, don't start. We came here to cheer you up and see how you're gettin' along before we all take off outta here. I'm leavin' soon, you're leavin' soon, and Joe's leavin'. Who knows when we'll see each other again, and for how long?"

"Dex," Kirby started laughing softly, "you gettin' misty on us?"

Dexter took a pillow and smashed Kirby, sending him flat on his bed. "I ain't gettin' misty. I'm just gonna miss you guys, that's all."

"Aw, th-th-that's—"

"Don't start, Joe, don't you start," Dexter said.

The well-disposed friends watched the remaining bits of *The Julia Show* and chatted casually, until Dexter remembered something. "Guess what," he said with visible excitement. "Guess what. Good news!"

"What! What, already." Kirby said.

"Simon got arrested the other day."

"What!"

"Yeah, the man is doin' time right now in Sing Sing."

"What did he do?"

"He punched out a cop."

"Get outta here. Which cop? What happened?"

"You know the cop. He's stationed on Gramatan Avenue," Dexter said, snapping his fingers, trying to remember the officer's name. "What's his name?"

"Of-Of-Officer Ja-Ja-Jack Rhoden."

"Yeah, Joe, him. Well—"

"He's a racist," Kirby said. "He did the city a favor. He—"

"Let me tell you what happened," Dexter said and stood up to demonstrate the act he'd witnessed. "Policeman Rhoden saw Simon's car. Simon had double-parked and apparently gone inside Ricky's Donut shop, but he put his hazard lights on."

"He was drivin'? Where was Willie?"

"I don't know, but Simon was alone. Anyway, Rhoden saw him go inside, but he waited until Simon came out to start writin' him a ticket. Simon didn't protest. He took it in stride and put his hand out for the ticket. But Rhoden snatched it back and started walkin' around the car. I guess he was checkin' for violations or somethin'. But he didn't find anything, so he came back to Simon and shoved the ticket in his chest. Then here's the kicker," Dexter started laughing. "He called him the dreaded "N" word."

"What? He called him a Negro?"

"No man, not that "N" word. Da udda one. And for good measure, he added that he was a lowdown and dirty one. He called him a dirty ni—"

"Get outta here."

"I kid you not. Man ... Simon dropped him somethin' serious though. I mean, he had Rhoden on queer street."

"What are you talkin' about?" Kirby asked.

Dexter and Big Joe started chortling uncontrollably as Dexter tried to get the words out. Kirby, too, started cackling even though he didn't know what the joke was all about.

"Well," Dexter managed to say, "just before Rhoden went out cold, he hit the ground, rolled over, and started yellin' and screamin', 'Where's my badge! Where's my badge!' Then he cried out for his Momma."

"What?"

"Kirby, I hadn't laughed so hard in years."

"What did Simon do?"

"Check this out. He lit up a cigar."

"Get out."

"Just like Red Auerbach does when he wins a championship, and just sat on top of his hood, waitin' for the cops to come. He didn't even try to run or get away. And I heard Rhoden's jaw is broken in three places."

"Man," Kirby said nonchalantly, "I guess I would've ended up in jail, too."

"Kirby, I thought you'd be jumpin' for joy about it. Simon's finally in the clink. The joint! The hoosegow! Up the river! The big house! And he's gonna do some serious time, man. He's lookin' at five to ten at least. You're not happy? I thought you'd be overjoyed."

Kirby had been staring down at his pillow. He elevated his head and said, "You say he's in Sing Sing, right?"

"What's wrong with you? You find religion on us, Kirby. You gone soft in your old age?"

"No, Dex. I guess I didn't tell you exactly everything that happened at Slappy's." Kirby proceeded to explain the whole ordeal to Joe and Dex.

They came away equally impressed with Simon and felt sorry for the way they'd been gloating over his situation.

******

Kirby woke up the next morning, feeling much better, so he decided to do some much-needed ripping and running. He stopped by a pawn shop and selected a set of wedding rings for himself and Kathy. He stopped by the Naval recruiter's office to finalize the paperwork. He also dropped by his mother's place of employment, Sears department store, and delivered her a dozen roses for her fiftieth birthday.

But Kirby's day wasn't done. He boarded a bus to Ossining, New York, the location of Sing Sing Prison. The place Simon would have to call home for a while.

He knew permission to see him as a regular off-the-street visitor would be prohibited. Since Simon had no idea to put him on the list, he used another method. Kirby knew one of the correction officers from their days at the Boys & Girls Club. Albeit he was much older, having graduated Mount Vernon High School in 1965, but he figured the club connection would suffice and make the officer willing to do him a solid and look out for a brother.

It worked. Kirby had to pose as Simon's son from California who'd come to New York, looking for his father. After being fingerprinted and going through the usual process of strip searching, Kirby took his place behind the telephone and two-way glass and awaited Simon's arrival.

The visiting room was painted a cold light green. The paint was not only cold, it was chipped, giving the room even more of an unwelcoming atmosphere. There were ten visiting stations equipped with cushioned chairs, ashtrays, and telephones. The high-glass blockade made any physical contact impossible. A guard patrolled the premises to keep order and to make sure none of the prisoners got out of hand with their emotions.

A half hour passed, and a surprised Simon arrived, clad in orange prison fatigues. He picked up the telephone and motioned to Kirby to do likewise.

"I'm glad to see you, but what're you doing here? And how did you get in?"

"I pulled a few strings. I know a few people around here. But I came to see how you were doin'. How you comin' along?"

Simon sat back in his seat and unleashed a colossal smile. "I've had better days. I'm not exactly used to this. Being confined and all, but I'm coming along. I'm coming along just fine. Thanks for asking."

Kirby had put his head down, fighting for words to say.

Simon noticed the anguish on Kirby's face and decided he'd help him along. "Is there something you want to say to me? I mean, you have this look on your face like you're constipated."

Kirby raised his head and managed a smile. "Yeah, Simon. I never thought I'd be tellin' you this, but I'm grateful, and I want to thank you for comin' to my aid. You saved my life, and I appreciate it."

"I told you before that he took the bullets out, didn't I?"

"Yeah, but as scared as I was, I could've died from a heart attack."

"Okay, now that your life has been saved, what're you gonna do with it?"

"What do you mean?"

"I mean are you gonna make something out of yourself or you gonna end up like me. Those streets don't have anything for you. Trust me."

Kirby had a bemused look on his face.

"It's me talking, from my mouth to your ears. What're you gonna do with yourself?"

"I can't believe you're talkin' like this. I mean, you?"

"Young fella, there's a lot about me you don't know. You probably wouldn't believe it anyway."

A curious Kirby said, "Try me."

"Some other time. Some other time. Listen," Simon pointed at Kirby, "take my advice. Stop what you're doing. I'm talking about the drinking and whatnot." He paused a moment as if a beam of light had shined upon him, then continued. "You didn't take the smack you bought the other day, did you?"

Kirby gave Simon another bemused look.

"Yeah, young fella, I knew about it also. And you won't have to worry about him selling anymore in Mount Vernon. Stop the nonsense and go to college or something. Get outta town for a while. Give yourself a chance, man. Do the right thing."

"I enlisted in the Navy."

"There's a war going on. There are other options, you know."

"I know, but I'll take my chances. Besides, I don't think the Navy will see too much action, if any. I'm man enough to handle whatever comes."

Kirby and Simon conversed a little while longer, switching subjects several times. Kirby urged Simon to seek help from witnesses. After all, he knew Dexter was there and had seen what'd happened.

Simon refused. He felt there was no chance of winning despite who saw what. He pressed on the fact of not being considered a community role model. He also cited that especially in Dexter's case, he was getting ready for college, and going back and forth to court for someone he'd once hated wouldn't be the wise thing to do. He intimated that he was man enough to take whatever came his way. He was ready to take his medicine and his punishment. He knew his lawyer would do all he could, but he expected the worst. He conceded that breaking a cop's jaw wasn't something that was okay to do.

Kirby lost track of the time while sitting and chatting with his newfound friend. Moments later, a guard declared that visiting hours were over.

"You gonna be all right, man?" Kirby asked with genuine concern.

"I'll be fine, young fella. You make sure you take care of yourself."

The guard impatiently tapped Kirby on his shoulder.

"I guess I better get outta here. Take care of yourself, Simon. I'll keep in touch."

"Okay, that'll be cool. And I'll do the same. Hey, congratulations on your upcoming wedding. I wish you all the best. Really."

Kirby got up and made his way toward the door. A tapping sound caused Kirby to stop. It was Simon frantically pounding on the glass.

Kirby looked at the guard, who was dressed in a blue uniform, readied with a gun, night stick, and handcuffs, to get his approval. The guard, reading Kirby's thoughts, frowned momentarily, as Kirby was the last one to leave. The guard reluctantly but affirmatively nodded.

Kirby went back to the station and picked up the telephone. "What's up, Simon?"

Simon, filled with emotion, put a fist up against the glass. Kirby followed suit, solidifying the bond between them.

"Thanks for coming to see about me. I really appreciate it. You really didn't have to do it."

"No problem."

"Promise me something." Simon looked Kirby straight in the eye. "I know I said this before to you, but I mean it. I want you to make something of yourself. Do you hear me? Make something of yourself."

"I will, Simon. I will. I promise."

CHAPTER ELEVEN

"Simon, you ready yet?" Kirby said as he, Kirby Jr., and Bennie entered his office. "The game starts in forty-five minutes. I don't want to miss the tipoff."

Simon was on the telephone, and from the looks of things, the conversation seemed to be very serious.

Kirby caught the hint of Simon's look and pushed his sons outside the door. "You guys go shoot some baskets until we're ready."

"Aw, Dad, come on," Junior said. He was the spitting image of his father—head shape, body structure, and nose—but had his mother's light brown eyes. "Do we have to?"

"Yeah, you have to. Now go on."

As the boys exited, Kirby focused his attention back on Simon, who was still engrossed in heavy dialog.

After several more minutes, Simon disconnected the call, then motioned for Kirby to shut the door. "That was Harry Hooch. The guy I was telling you about who could dig up some stuff about Bennett's murder."

"Yeah," an eager Kirby answered. "What's up? What does he have for us?"

"Kirby, as I suspected all along, Bennett was the victim of a hit. A hired, high-priced hit. Nothing the average person could afford. It had to be out-of-towners 'cause I didn't hear anything about it on the streets."

"What!" A chill ran through Kirby as he sat down.

"Just as I suspected way back when," Simon chimed in. "I'm sorry."

Kirby ran his hands through his hair and massaged his face before responding, "Who? Why?

Who on earth would put out a hit like that on a high school kid? I mean, Bennett, he wasn't into anything that'd necessitate being taken out."

"Listen ... Harry may be onto something. He doesn't have any names yet, but he feels he's getting close. The reason I was talking to him so long is because he was advising me as to what I—I mean, *we* should do in the meantime."

"What does he have in mind?"

"You're not gonna like this, but he said we should seek the help of the mayor."

Kirby made a gesture with his head that clearly displayed his dismay over the idea. But before he could get the word *no* out of his mouth, Simon reminded him that the idea was to find Bennett's killer, not to make friends. After careful thought, Kirby knew giving in was the best thing. The two men agreed but decided to table the strategy discussion for later.

Suddenly, Kirby's kids crashed into the office. "Dad, let's go!" Junior said. "We're gonna miss the start of the most important game of the year!"

"We only have twenty minutes," Bennie said.

"I know, son," Kirby said with a sly grin. "Mount Vernon verses New Ro. Survival of the fittest. Best man wins. It's not just war ... it's Armageddon."

"Daddy," Bennie said, not appreciating being teased.

"Hey, guys. I was on the team before, remember?"

"That was so long ago, Daddy. Things are different now."

Simon and Kirby looked at one another and exchanged grins. Simon gave Kirby the signal to keep quiet, as he didn't feel much like a huge debate.

And being cognizant of the time and importance of the game to his kids, Kirby decided to leave it alone and made his way to his car with Simon and the boys. Then off they went to the Mount Vernon High School gymnasium.

The high school parking lot was full of loud cheers even though the game hadn't begun. The intensity level was as thick as the darkness of night.

The moment Kirby purchased the tickets, a surge went through his body. He couldn't be sure if it was from the unnerving news he'd learned about Bennett or the excitement about the game. He tried to put the information about Bennett behind him for the time being. But it was utterly impossible, because after a twelve-year absence, he'd returned to the gym where Bennett made his name.

Apart from a new paint job, Kirby saw that the place still looked the same. The banner for the 1973 championship, which Bennett single-handedly won, hung high on the wall to the left of the gym's entrance. And he noticed the school had retired Bennett's number, 42.

The crowd was heading to their seats as the cheerleaders from both schools shouted rah-rah chants to one another. Town political figures from both cities, including the mayors, were in attendance. Among the assemblage of students and townspeople, college and NBA scouts could be spotted, jotting notes.

The game was set to start in a matter of minutes, so both teams were warming up with layup drills. But out of all the players, Dannon was absolutely marvelous. He was wreaking havoc, putting on a dunking exhibition that would've made Dr. J envious. He was coming down on the hoop so strong that the basket would shake uncontrollably for several seconds after he'd left his mark. The loud thud he made upon his descent would startle inattentive fans.

At last, the showdown was about to begin.

This game wasn't for all the marbles, but it was for a whole bunch of them and bragging rights. Both teams were destined to make the playoffs. They each carried undefeated records going into the game. Mount Vernon with ten wins, and New Rochelle with eleven.

The ten combatants met at the circle of honor and exchanged the traditional handshakes. It was obvious though that these guys really didn't care for each other. Dannon made his way over to New Rochelle's star power forward and defensive whiz, Chandler McMurtry. He stood a rugged six-foot-seven and 210 pounds. He was probably a tad shorter than that, but because he sported one of those hi-lo fade haircuts, it was hard to actually tell.

The rest of McMurtry's crew consisted of the six-foot-three, point guard supreme, Gregory Starks, and the All-County shooting guard, six-foot-four Nick "Mercedes" Benns. Josh Baxter, at six-foot-nine, was the big man in the middle, and six-foot-five small forward O'Brien O'Hara O'Sullivan, aka Triple O-Seven.

No fooling, that was his name. His parents, Oliver and Olga, had this fascination with names that started with the letter "O".

The Mount Vernon quintet was no slouch either. Dannon had plenty of firepower to go along with him. His best friend, Jordan "Fleet Feet" Alexander, was the point guard. At six-foot-four, he was considered the quickest and the strongest point guard in the state.

Manual Rivera, at six-foot-one, played out of position at the shooting guard spot. Handling the basketball wasn't his forte, but because of his sweet shooting stroke, Coach Dee had put him in the starting lineup.

The center, Ranfi Hutu, at six-foot-ten, manned, controlled, and policed the paint area. He averaged an unprecedented twelve blocks per game to go along with eighteen rebounds.

Rounding out the top five was fellow all-state honoree, six-foot-six small forward Ray Richardson.

"McMurtry," Dannon said as he was tying a knot into his uniform short pants, "I hear you been talkin' trash in the paper about how you're gonna hold me to ten points. Is that right?"

"Yeah." McMurtry rose to his feet to look Dannon straight in the eye. "I believe I said somethin' to that effect. I don't see where I was misquoted."

"Well, did you mean ten points for the game or for the first quarter. I think your mouth may be writin' checks your behind can't cash."

"What a wonderful saying. Did your Momma teach you that?"

Dannon lost his cool and had to be restrained by Jordan Alexander.

"Don't get yourself kicked outta the game on my account. Stay awhile and take the whoopin' like a man. Or lady, whatever you prefer."

"What's all the conversation about?" the ref said. "Let's play ball!"

Dannon was fuming and couldn't wait until the ref threw the ball up.

The ref did his part, and Mount Vernon took control. Jordan handed the ball off to Dannon, who immediately called for a clear-out play. McMurtry jumped into his trademark defensive stance and began yelling some unpleasant things at him. Dannon somehow kept his poise despite the force of adrenaline eating away at him.

With a head movement, he faked left and went right with a speed dribble. After shifting his bodyweight, McMurtry smiled and caught up to Dannon, again, yelling harsh things at him. Dannon bounced the ball between his legs in a stutter step, crossover dribble fashion and juke faked again.

McMurtry went flying past Dannon, but not before Dannon told him, "Have a nice flight, baby." Then he swished home a jump shot.

On defense, Dannon called Ray Richardson off. He wanted to guard McMurtry.

Coach Dee knew of Dannon's competitive fire but couldn't care less, so long as he stayed within the team concept. Dannon was careful not to get in a heavy trash-talking episode. Not with the horde of scouts in the stands watching his every move.

"I got him, Ray, take mine!" Dannon kept his eyes trained on him.

He got posted up by McMurtry on the left baseline. Someone yelled, "I got your help," as McMurtry tried to create space for himself. Dannon refused it, as he had his own plan for defending.

Dannon waited until McMurtry felt comfortable in his post position, then faked like he'd been beaten and backed away lamely. Instantly, McMurtry squared up to take his shot, but Dannon suddenly appeared out of nowhere and pinned the rising shot against the backboard. The force of the block was so great that during a timeout, Jordan told Dannon that he thought he'd heard air seep out of the ball.

Mount Vernon was back on offense. Jordan yelled out the Three-Down power play, which called for Dannon to post up his man on the right box once everyone cleared out.

Dannon took a deep breath and readied himself to receive the pass. The moment he got the ball, you could hear the fierce rumble of the crowd. Fans, in anticipation of something great, started stomping their feet in a stampede-like fashion. The sound of the earthquake had the building rocking.

Dannon asked his defender, Chandler McMurtry, "You got me, boy?"

"I'm in your back pocket, son. Bring it on."

Dannon obliged. He head-faked left and drop-stepped right. McMurtry, in one fell swoop, hit the floor as if someone had clocked him. Dannon peered briefly at his fallen foe as he ascended. Upon reaching his peak, he cocked the ball behind his head and slammed it through the hoop.

The New Rochelle coach felt he was losing his team and was compelled to call a timeout.

The onslaught continued, with Mount Vernon winning the game 101-78. Dannon ended the game with forty-seven points, fifteen rebounds, and ten assists. And what shouldn't be lost is that Dannon, after he'd stripped McMurtry of the ball at least a dozen times, held him to only eight points.

At the game's final buzzer, while the Mount Vernon fans were going wild, McMurtry made his way over to Dannon and allowed good sportsmanship to take over. After all, they were one-time teammates on the Westchester County AAU basketball team. Dannon wished him luck throughout the rest of their season, except if they met again, of course.

Kirby sat in the stands, overcome with emotion. He felt all the virtue of the team's win as if he were a direct part of it himself. He hugged and hi-fived his two sons to death.

Suddenly, a sharp pain pierced through his head, which was so severe that he felt himself becoming faint.

Dannon was making his way to the locker room when Jay Rock, who was with two of his comrades, yelled something to him. Dannon changed courses and proceeded over to him.

Simon saw that and told Kirby he'd be back. "Jay Rock," Simon said, giving him a menacing look. "Now I told you before ..."

"Simon, slow down. I was just tellin' him nice game, that's all."

"What's goin' on, Simon?" a befuddled Dannon asked.

"Nothing. How you gettin' home?"

"Momma and I are gettin' a ride with Aunt Traci."

"Okay, go on and get yourself changed, and I'll see you tomorrow," Simon said, exchanging dirty looks with Jay Rock and his partners as he shoved Dannon away.

One of Jay Rock's companions whispered something in his ear, and the two started snickering.

As Simon walked away, he caught Junior flailing his arms frantically and shot up the bleachers like a cannon. "Kirby, you all right?"

"The pain in my head. It's killing me, Simon."

"I'm taking you to the hospital. I'm not waiting for an ambulance."

"Wait a second. I don't want anybody to see me like this."

"We're parked in the back. Let's go out the back door. Come on, man, I got you."

The ride to the Mount Vernon hospital was a blur, as Simon took every light and ran every stop sign in his path.

When Kirby came to, he found himself on his back, stretched out on a gurney with a doctor's bright flashlight shining in his eyes.

"Can you hear, son?" the doctor asked. "You're in the emergency room."

Kirby's eyes were unfocused as his mind wandered. He began to have the same sickening feeling he'd experienced when Bennett lay bleeding profusely from his bullet wound.

"I can hear you." Just as Kirby answered, he heard someone to his left sniffling. He turned to see who it was and saw it was his wife. "Kathy, what're you doing here? And where are the kids?"

Kathy took time to wipe her face and gather herself before answering. "Simon took them home and put them to bed. We didn't think they should be here."

"You guys didn't call my mother, did you?"

"Of course, we did. We had to. And she's on her way over. She should be here any minute."

"Don't get yourself excited, son. Relax." The doctor removed his thick bifocal glasses.

Kirby thought, *Either the man got dressed in the dark, or those glasses aren't doin' any good.*

The doctor was dressed in black-, white-, and green-striped psychedelic pants and a red and blue pin-striped shirt.

Another doctor, who was dressed a lot more civilized and looked to be in his late fifties, entered the area, carrying an X-ray result from a CAT scan. "Hi, Mr. Maxwell."

"Call me Kirby."

"Okay, Kirby," the doctor obliged as he looked at Kathy. "I'm sorry, are you his wife? Please ... don't get up."

"Yes, she's my wife. Her name is Kathy."

"Well, my name is Dr. Lewis. Dr. Jonathan Lewis. Kirby, I'm going to cut to the chase," he said matter-of-factly. "You nearly had a stroke. And you very well could've died from a brain aneurysm. Simply put, you were at death's door. I know it sounds scary, especially given your age, but it's true. You have to, I mean absolutely have to slow yourself down. I don't know what your personal life is like, but whatever it is, it's not worth dying for. Slow down."

"Oh, my God," Kathy said.

"You should be pretty much out of danger now. We were able to drain most of the fluid. But you might feel a little woozy or drunk because you're sedated enough where you won't feel any pain. The rest of the rehabilitation process now begins with you."

"A stroke? How? Why? But ..."

Dr. Lewis displayed the X-ray to Kirby and Kathy. He then asked Kirby if he ever remembered being struck on the head, or if he was in an accident where his neck or spine could've been injured.

Kirby thought a moment, then remembered Shorty hitting him in the head with a pool stick and being thrown against a wall headfirst. Dr. Lewis then provided him and Kathy with an explanation. He cited that although the incident happened several years ago, the stress and strain he'd experienced had caused fluid to build on the brain. Calcification—swelling on the brain—was the medical term he used. It had happened at the spot where the skull was chipped by the blow he'd taken. Dr. Lewis referred to it as the reason for the blurred vision and migraines.

The news hit Kirby like a ton of bricks. But he felt grateful to his son Junior for sounding the alarm to Simon, who'd rushed him to the hospital. Simon had saved his life a second time, and he hadn't paid him back yet for the first.

The doctors left but not before telling Kirby that he'd have to spend a few days in the hospital and follow instructions. He agreed.

Kathy grabbed her saddened and teary-eyed husband by the hand and rubbed it gently.

"Sweetie, why don't you come back home now," she said delicately.

"Kathy—"

"We miss you so much. I miss you so much. You are my soulmate, Kirby, and I love you."

"Kathy, I don't know about it right now. We argue too much. I mean, that's all we ever do—argue, argue, argue. I can't take the stress of it anymore. I just can't."

"Who's gonna take care of you?"

"I'm not crippled or incapacitated. I'm just hurt, and I have to take it easy. I've been ready to leave IBM anyway. I'm ready to start my own consulting operation. I have enough money put away in case I had to take a loss for a while.

But I have a lot of contacts, so it shouldn't be too long of a wait."

"Kirby—"

"Kathy, please," Kirby covered his eyes to lessen the pain. He just didn't want to talk about it anymore.

Just as the conversation ended, Kirby's mother walked in. "Son. Baby, are you all right? What happened?"

"Yes, Momma, I'm fine. Momma, calm down. I'm fine. I'm outta danger."

"What did they do to your head? What's all these bandages?"

"They—"

"Oh, Kathy, sugar, Momma's sorry. How are you?" Lois said and kissed her on the forehead.

"I'm fine, thank you."

"Tell me what's happening?" Lois demanded again and got the full explanation from Kathy.

Lois was pressed to the limit not to go to Shorty's house, providing she could find it, and smash him in the head with an object.

Kirby urged his mother not to waste her time trying to look for him. Shorty was about to do time. Five to ten for armed robbery.

"Son, I told you, you need to take it easy. Can't save the world."

"Momma, I know. I'll take it easy."

"Promise me, Kirby," Lois said, imploring him to respond with the answer she wanted to hear. "Promise me."

"I promise."

"Say it again." Lois looked him up and down. "And don't cross your fingers or toes. I know your little tricks. I raised you."

"Yes, Momma, I won't forget."

CHAPTER TWELVE

Kirby pressed the *off* button on his remote as he went to answer the knock on the door. It was Simon, holding a large bag of Chinese food.

"Smells good, man," Kirby said as he took the bag off Simon's hands and placed it on his kitchen table. "What'cha got here?"

\"Just a little Egg Foo Yo/ 7ung from General Tso's Chicken. A little broccoli and rice, some spareribs, some pork fried rice, and some moo goo guy pan."

"You got enough, Simon? Who're we feeding, Pharaoh's army?"

"Ay." Simon patted Kirby on the shoulder before having a sit-down on the couch. "Whatever we don't eat, you keep."

Simon and Kirby chowed down and chatted easily well into the wee hours of the night. Then the subject of Bennett came up again, much like it always did.

"I still want to find Bennett's killer."

"Didn't the doctor tell you that you have to take things easy? It's only been a week since you've seen him."

Kirby gave Simon a look that made Simon hold his ears and say, "Don't say it. My virgin ears can't take it."

"Oh, stop it. What did Harry Hooch say?"

"Forget him for now. We have a meeting with Sol tomorrow at his office. I've been speaking with him off and on. He's talking about re-opening the case."

"Forget it ..."

"I'll pick you up tomorrow morning at 9:00. Be dressed and ready to go. But if I have to drag you outta bed tomorrow, I will."

******

Tomorrow came but not a second too soon for Kirby. He hated to see the man who'd married his deceased buddy's girlfriend. He disapproved of the way it was done. But for Bennett's sake, and not his own, he willed himself into getting ready for the meeting. Besides, he felt himself grow queasy at the thought of Simon having to dress him.

He met Simon at the appointed time in front of his building, and the ride to City Hall was a breeze. Outside, City Hall had this old-time colonial look, and inside was made up of all marble and brass. It had a spiral staircase in the middle of it that led directly to the mayor's chambers.

Simon and Kirby followed the stairway path as if they were Dorothy, the Tin-Man, and the Cowardly Lion in the Wizard of Oz following the yellow brick road. When they reached the mayor's office, Kirby begrudgingly asked the receptionist for Sol, and Simon had to elbow him.

"Come on, Simon. It's not like I want to be here anyway."

"I know that, but he's our link right now."

Sol was expecting them, but they had to wait until Sol was done with his morning jog. Before the two took their seats, Simon advised Kirby not to mention anything about Harry Hooch and his contacts.

Kirby hated being there but was quite impressed with the way Sol's digs looked.

It had a thick green rug that made you feel like you were walking on air. The chairs were dark brown with thick leather padding. The huge maple wood desk had a sheet of glass covering it, which made the place glisten with even more class. All the pictures on the wall were either framed or lamented. And the office had a nice, fresh air odor to it.

A half-hour passed before Sol showed. He'd showered and changed his clothes beforehand. "Gentlemen." He walked in arrayed in a blue pin-striped suit, white shirt, and blue paisley tie. "How are you?"

Sol wasn't only the first Jewish man elected to head the City of Mount Vernon, he was also the youngest, at thirty-one.

Simon shook his hand immediately. Kirby reneged, leaving Sol hanging with his hand out. Simon again nudged him. This time with much more force.

"Yeah, how are you, Sol. Long time."

"I've been fine, and yourself?"

"Peachy ... just dandy."

Simon shook his head and said to himself, *You're gonna blow it, Kirby. You're gonna blow it.*

"How's Tara?" Simon asked and received a dirty look from Kirby.

Luckily, Sol had bent down behind his desk for something, or else he would've seen it and maybe changed his mind about helping them.

"Fine, just fine. As a matter of fact, she should be here any moment."

"She's coming here?" Kirby asked hostilely.

"Yes. She'd like to see you. She hasn't seen you in almost ten years."

"Ten years too soon," Kirby mumbled.

"I'm sorry, Kirby. Did you say something?"

"No, I didn't say anything. I was just thinking out loud."

Sol and Simon began conversing about Simon's mayoralty, his family, and his aspirations in politics. He had his sights set on a congressional or senatorial seat, a gubernatorial ticket, and eventually, a presidential one.

The tête-à-tête was boring Kirby, and he started to feel left out. He let out a loud sigh, and Simon knew to change gears.

"Sol, we better get this ball rolling," Simon said, attempting to calm Kirby down.

"Yes, yes, of course." Sol flipped through some papers on his desk. "So, you guys wish to re-open Bennett's murder case?"

"Re-open? Re-open? The case should never have been closed. The killer was never caught."

"I'm sorry, Kirby. That's what I meant."

Just then, there was a knock at the door, and an abrupt entrance was made. It was the very tall and slender Mount Vernon Chief of Police, Caption Floral Demetry Turner. The man with the whitest hair on the face of the earth. The man that had the nerve to one day try and dye it black. To which the nickname Captain Piano Head was born.

He exchanged greetings with Simon and Kirby before making his way over to Sol to hand him a file folder and whisper in his ear. He made his exit just as quickly but not before nodding at Simon and Kirby.

Kirby felt the whole shebang had gone wrong, judging by the way Sol sat in his chair and fumbled with his pencil.

"Sol ..."

"His file is missing."

"I knew it was too good to be true. I knew something would go wrong." Kirby slapped the arm of the chair. "Missing!"

"Yeah," Simon added. "Missing. I don't understand. You knew I ... I mean, *we* were coming. How could the files be missing?"

"As you know, the case was quite some time ago. I don't know, perhaps things were just transferred over somewhere without proper documentation to trace it. But don't worry, I promise we'll find it. We'll keep on top of it. It's a high-priority matter."

Kirby had all he could stand and headed for the door. Simon had little choice but to follow suit. They came together. They had to leave together. They rode in Kirby's car.

"Wait fellas, please. I have good news. I mean really good news. You want to hear this."

"You have a suspect?" Kirby said.

Sol propelled himself from behind his desk and made his way toward the door to meet with the two men. He then responded, "No, it's not that."

"Well, what kind of good news would you possibly have at this point. Come on, Sol. Don't waste my time, and please don't toy with me."

"I assure you, I'm not toying with you, Kirby. Trust me. Please sit and hear me out."

Kirby and Simon looked at one another to force an approval. Giving Sol the benefit of doubt, they sat, not too trustfully, to hear what Sol had to say.

The news he had for them was that Mount Vernon was planning to give Bennett a day.

The high school was going to induct Bennett into its Alumni Hall of Fame. And through donations and other sources, the high school was going to have a scholarship in Bennett's name in the amount of $25,000. The award would be given annually and dispersed among two hundred students.

And as more monies came in, the more students that would benefit.

They were also informed by Sol that the Fourth Street Playground as they presently knew it would be no more. The new name would be the Bennett Wilson Memorial Playground. And an annual basketball summer league would be held in his memory. It would be dubbed the Bennett Wilson Memorial Open Invitational Tournament.

The news brought a big smile to Kirby's face. He nearly jumped out of his seat. But that wasn't all, Sol insisted. The playground, after a groundbreaking memorial ceremony, would be re-done with new tarp, new basketball goals, a new volleyball setup, and brand-new plastic bleachers. Something that would be able to withstand the constant change of the weather.

But the gem of them all, Sol added, would be something really special. Kirby and Simon thought, *Wow, how more special can it get?* Sol picked up a box, pulled out a bronze statue, and handed it over to Kirby. Kirby was dumbfounded but was too excited about everything to ask any questions.

Sol said he was going to finance the sculpturing of a ten-foot statue of Bennett to be placed directly in front of the high school. He said that Bennett would be holding books with his left hand. Under his right foot, he'd be holding a basketball, and his right hand would point upward. Sol also added that words would be engraved on it. Something to the effect of, REACH HIGH, AIM HIGH, SOAR HIGH. THE SKY IS YOUR LIMIT.

He felt those would be appropriate words coming from the mouth of Bennett, and Kirby couldn't have agreed with him more as he beamed with excitement. He was so overcome with joy that he felt guilty for slugging Sol and smashing his glasses twelve years ago.

Sol gathered himself and told the two buddies that everything would take place in June, the second week after school officially let out. It was a five-month wait, and Kirby could hardly stand it.

"So, how's Ms. Wilson taking all of?"

"Kirby, the woman cried for two days she was so happy. But she's still smiling, and rightfully so. She deserves it. Bennett deserves it. Hey, Mount Vernon has got to honor its own. Bennett was and still is an inspiration to us all. We've all learned something from him. Let's honor him."

"Sol, I'm sorry for everything I've done. I mean ..."

"Ay ... forget it," Sol said with a laugh.

Another greeter was at the door. This time, the party waited for someone to ask who it was before entering.

It was Tara, and she was good and pregnant. The smile on Kirby's face quickly vanished. His emotions were going crazy. He was ecstatic about Bennett's upcoming tributes but seeing Bennett's ex impregnated by Sol bothered him.

Tara still looked the same as in high school. She was still fine. She still had that soft, caramel-complexioned skin and those same chubby cheeks that dimpled whenever she smiled. Her body was a little—or rather, a lot—disfigured, but it was to be expected given her condition.

"How are you, Simon?" Tara kissed him on the cheek. "And how are you, Mr. Kirby?" Her smile widened as she kissed Kirby also.

"I've been okay. How've you been?"

Kirby's stomach knotted with anger as he watched Tara and Sol exchange kisses on the mouth. But he really got perturbed when he noticed Tara continuously pat on her belly while making conversation.

"How are Kitty Kat and the boys doing?"

"Everyone's fine, thanks. I'll tell them you sent your best."

"Please do." Tara sat down in an exhausted fashion. "Tell her I'm going to be a mommy in two months, and I want her to come to my shower."

"Whoa, look at the time." Kirby attempted to end the conversation. "We better get outta here, Simon."

"Won't you guys stay for lunch?"

"Naw, we won't, Sol. Sorry. But we'll definitely keep in touch. If you find those files, or if you guys come up with something, please inform me. I need to know. I still ... you know."

"Yeah, I know." The two gentlemen shook hands. "I know."

Simon and Kirby were back in the hallway where it all started. And not a moment too soon for Kirby's taste.

"Man, am I glad to be outta there! Where to now?"

Simon smiled as he put his arm around his friend and led him down the steps. "Next stop, the cemetery."

"Cemetery?"

"Yeah, I thought I told you it was Wanda's birthday and I wanted to lay some flowers down for her."

"No, I don't recall. But I'll go. And this way, I can holler at Bennett and tell him the good news."

"I'm sure he'd like it."

Simon knelt, laid a bushel of flowers by Wanda's tombstone, and said a prayer. Suddenly, he was submerged under a dark shadow. He got to his feet to gain back some sunlight and to see who was towering over him.

"Can I help you, young man?" Simon said.

"Who are you?" the rugged-looking young man with the deep penetrating voice said in response.

"I'm Simon. Who are you?"

The young man then plucked out his toothpick and showed off his pearly whites mixed with gold and said, "I'm Wanda's younger brother, Wesley."

"Whoa, Wesley," Simon said and stuck out his hand. "Glad to meet you. I knew your sister."

"I know." Wesley squeezed Simon's hand so hard the blood left it. Simon had to use his other hand to pry it away.

"I'm glad to finally meet you also. Finally." Wesley walked off, whistling the melody of the Pink Panther cartoon.

Kirby approached Simon from behind as he watched Wesley stroll down the hill.

"Man, you scared me," Simon said, continuing to flex his hand to get the blood circulating again.

"Who was the mountain man?"

Simon hesitated before answering. So much so, Kirby had to ask him a second time.

"Oh, he-he-he was ... *is* Wanda's brother. He said he was Wanda's brother."

Kirby saw the care-worn look on Simon's face and felt compassion for him. "You nervous a little bit."

"For some reason, I'm not just nervous. I'm a little frightened. Just a little though. But frightened nonetheless."

"Don't worry, I got your back."

Simon displayed a fake smile and playfully slapped Kirby on the chest with his gloves. "Let's go see Harry Hooch."

CHAPTER THIRTEEN

"Harry Ho! Harry Ho! Harry Ho! Harry Hooch! Where you be, son! Come out! Come out! Wherever you are!" Simon yelled as he and Kirby walked up the squeaking steps of the dilapidated tenement in the roughest section of Mount Vernon.

The stairwell stunk something fierce. So much so, it took Kirby's breath away. Somehow, Simon refused to mind. In fact, he seemed more inclined to wallow in it, proclaiming, "Sol's office should smell this good."

"Shhh! Simon, come here," Harry Hooch said and motioned the two inside his cat-infested apartment.

"Look at all these cats." Kirby dodged across the floor to keep from stepping on one.

"Don't worry, they're just here to keep me company and to keep the mice and roaches away."

"There's a better way," Simon chimed in, and the two men hugged. "How you doin', man?"

"I can't complain," Harry said as he took in another puff of his Winston-Salem. "Well, actually I can, but who'd listen?"

Harry was short, hairy, and scruffy looking. He had so much hair on his body, it was hard to determine his ethnicity. The hair on his head was jet black and long. He always donned a hat of some kind and dark shades, even while in-doors. He smoked cigarettes like they were going out of style, and his attire always had to have some black in it. He was superstitious that way.

"I'll listen to you, Bra. You know you can count on me anytime."

Harry saw Kirby standing in the middle of the living room, seemingly afraid to sit down.

"Have a seat, young man."

"No!" Kirby looked down at the couch as if something was going to jump up and bite him. "I mean, no, it's all right."

"Please, have a seat. This is my home."

"No, I don't think so."

"Kirby," Simon said with authority, attempting to diffuse any tension that was in the air.

"How many cats do you have, Hooch?" Kirby asked.

"Harry. Call me Harry. And I have nine cats."

After sidestepping and dodging cats in his path, Kirby was prompted by Simon to discontinue insulting Harry, so he let his eyes and body language do the talking.

"Where'd you find this guy, Simon?"

"He's a good guy. He was Bennett's best friend. He's the guy I was telling you about that wanted all the information."

"Young fella," Harry said after taking a puff of his cancer stick, "you married?"

Kirby, somewhat taken aback by the question, offered, "No, I'm not, but my wife is."

"Simon!" an enraged Harry hollered. "Where'd you get this clown from?"

"Come on, Hooch, everything's cool."

Kirby then inexplicably reached inside his pocket and pulled out a roll of hundred-dollar bills and handed them to Harry.

"What's this?"

"Your fee," Kirby said matter-of-factly.

Harry looked at Simon, and Simon looked at Kirby.

No words were exchanged until Harry said to Simon, "You and I need to talk."

They got up to go to a back room. On the way, Simon went over to Kirby, who wore a dumbfounded look on his face.

"What I do? What I say?"

"He doesn't take money until the job is complete. He thinks it's a jinx for him to get paid beforehand."

"I don't know, Simon." Kirby shook his head. "That guy's one weird bird. And he's so hairy. He looks like a chia pet. And look ... look at this nasty house. It looks like somebody's backyard. Grass! Dirt! At least, I hope its dirt." He pointed at the brown substance at his feet.

"Ease up, man, relax. I think it's for the cats." Simon started for the back room as Harry called out again. "Anyway, I'll take care of everything. Why don't you help yourself to something in the fridge? Harry won't mind."

"You almost made me cuss. I don't care how much he feels insulted, I ain't eating or drinking nothing in here. The food would probably walk to me. And here, give him a breath mint."

"I'm coming, Harry! I'm coming!"

Kirby sat in absolute fear as the two men conferred in the back. He became even more creeped out when three cats descended upon him. One went for his feet. One went for his head, and another jumped on his lap. Kirby picked it up and threw it across the room. It landed safely on its feet.

Several minutes passed before the twosome reemerged. Harry made his way over to Kirby and stuck out his callous-ridden hand. Kirby looked at it carefully before relinquishing his. The two shook hands, and all was well again.

"Young fella, please forgive me. It's just I do business in a particular way. And sometimes it could lead to misunderstandings."

"Hey, I can dig it."

"Okay, now to the business at hand."

Harry went on about what he'd gathered through his contacts.

"Your friend Bennett was the victim of a hit. Someone put out a hit on him."

"What?" Kirby said, voice full of shock and amazement.

"Who paid the contract, I don't know. But whoever did had a lotta money. Either that or they had a lot of influence. The rifle used was no ordinary one.

"How do you know it was a rifle. I mean ...?"

Harry looked at Simon, and Simon immediately tapped Kirby on the shoulder, giving him the signal to shut up.

"I know by the bullet used that it was an assault rifle of some kind. And the barrel had been sawed off and switched. A common practice used by hitmen when they deal with gunsmiths on the take."

But with all the information gathered, not finding the trigger man or money person wasn't the most puzzling issue. The fact that someone had wanted to kill Bennett and the manner in which he died was most perplexing. Aside from a little street skirmish and minor disagreements, having someone taken out in broad daylight like that was very disconcerting.

Harry though, for all it was worth, vowed to get to the bottom of it. He believed he'd come up with names, faces, and places within ample time. Usually, whenever Harry said something, he meant it.

Four hours came and went before Simon peeked at his watch.

"Hooch, I'm outta here. I gotta go now." Simon noticed a mirthless look on Harry's hairy face.

"What's the matter, I'll keep in touch," he said with assuring laughter.

Harry's response prompted another voicing of concern from Simon. This time, with more sincerity. "Hey, Hooch. What's going on, man?"

"It's Little Tiny Smalls ..."

"Oh, yeah! How's my man doin'?"

Harry Hooch began to shake his head in a negative fashion. "It doesn't look good for him. Not good at all. He really wants to see you. He's in Bronx Lebanon Hospital."

"Hey, Hooch, man. Why didn't you tell me about this sooner? That's not right. You know how I feel about him. I love the guy ..."

"He wants to see you so that you can give him his last rites, Simon. You being the only preacher he really knows, let alone would trust."

"He's really that sick? What's wrong with him?"

"You'll have to see for yourself. Whatever it is though, it's got him. It's got him real good."

"Bronx Lebanon?"

"Yeah, he's in some special unit. You know, just ask for him, Lindsay Beale Donaldson, and they'll direct you there. Take young fella there with you."

"Why?"

"Trust me, you'll want to take him with you."

******

"Hi, I'd like to see Mister Lindsay Beale Donaldson," Simon said to the receptionist as he stood in the lobby of the Bronx Lebanon Hospital.

The hospital was different from the one in Mount Vernon.

The people weren't nearly as friendly, and the place seemed to be unkempt. More like, patients went there to die rather than to be cured.

"He's here. Unit 4A. Please take these visitors' passes."

"Thank you. Here, Kirby. Yours."

As Simon and Kirby strolled down the corridor en route to Little Tiny's room, all they could hear were sounds of agony coming from patients. Patients squealed as if being pierced with sharpened objects.

They reached Tiny's room, and a look of gloom splattered Simon's face after he saw Little Tiny Smalls. "Tiny?" Simon said, looking for a little assurance.

And how could he have been sure. He remembered Harry Hooch telling him how sick he was. But hearing how much his looks had changed wasn't the same as seeing it for himself.

Tiny once carried well over three hundred pounds. His weight was now was hovering around ninety pounds, and he appeared very weak. The black hair that once topped his skull had turned off-whitish and was reduced to spots and patches. The massive hands he used to have were small and frail looking. His fingernails were jet black. Most every tooth was missing. Those that remained were rotten to the core.

Kirby's head began to hurt, and he had to take a seat in the hall.

"Simon. My friend, you came to see about me?" Tiny said. You could tell every breath had become an ordeal for the man, who at one time was known to have the strength of Samson.

"Yeah, man. I would've come sooner, if only I'd known."

"You came at the right time, believe me. I'm so glad to see you. I see you have your young fella taggin' along with you."

"We were taking care of business together. How're you feeling?"

Tiny, who was hooked up to an intravenous feeder, began coughing uncontrollably and hacking up blood.

The sight frightened Simon terribly and he offered, "You want me to get the nurse?"

"No, no, this happens all the time. I'm used to it."

Simon started wiping Tiny's face with a towel when a nurse entered. "You can't handle the patients without gloves on."

"What?"

"Hospital rules, sir ... I'm sorry, sir."

"Rules? This is my friend. I'm not going to handle him with gloves. I'm not. I refuse."

"I'm sorry, sir," the pudgy nurse with the red hair and freckles said as she handed Simon a pair of gloves.

The two talked a while as Simon managed to become more comfortable with Tiny's condition. Reminiscing on old times seemed to put a smile on Tiny's face. But Simon sensed that Tiny was getting weary. "I better get going. I'll see you real soon. Probably Saturday."

"No, Kirby. You won't see me on Saturday."

"Why?" Simon asked, trying to give Tiny hope. "You leaving to go home? Home to a place where I won't find you? Harry Hooch will find you for me."

Tiny smiled a bit and stuck his hand out. Simon was reluctant to grab it for fear that he might hurt him.

"Simon, I have AIDS, and I don't think I'll make it to Saturday. I'm dying. I'm a dead man."

Tears of sorrow forced their way out of Simon's eyes and trickled down his face.

Kirby looked in through the glass window, saw him sobbing, and made his way back inside.

"Hey, young fella. How you doin'?"

"I'm fine, Tiny. I'm just fine."

"I'm cool, Kirby. Wait for me outside, thanks."

"You sure? Okay then, but I think I'll go down to the lobby and wait. Tiny, you take care of yourself and get well soon."

"Take care of yourself, young fella. Be good."

Simon tried to regain his composure so that he'd be able to speak intelligently. It was hard, but he managed.

"What do you mean, you have AIDS? You didn't go that way. I don't—"

"I was messing with one of my girls. She was infected. She was an IV drugger." Tiny's eyes became bloodshot as the pain seeped through his fragile body.

"Oh, Tiny," Simon said as tears began to flow again. "You knew the rules. We never mixed business with pleasure. Let alone not wearing a raincoat."

Tiny's cough came back again, and blood, saliva, and mucus accompanied it. Simon did as he'd done before and helped his friend.

"I know, but I took a liking to her."

"Is she still alive?"

"She died two years ago, not long after Big Willie passed. But she wasn't the only one I was with. So, I don't know."

Tiny spoke some more of his condition, and afterward, he pointed to his right arm.

"No, Tiny. You shot up, too? Were you trying to kill yourself, man?"

"No, Simon. I got reckless, and I got careless, that's all. I just got careless, and I didn't protect myself. And I'm going to die for it." Tiny's conversation was again interrupted by another series of whooping coughs accompanied by blood, saliva, and mucus. "Warn those kids you love so much. Warn them and use me for an example. Warn them." Tiny took some time to suck air. "Simon, I can't fight this. I can't fight this even with my stick."

The last remark garnered a slight smile from Simon. "I don't know what to do, Tiny."

"I want you to give me my last rites. I'm sure Hooch told you."

"Let's pray for healing instead."

"Simon, I wish I could. But I don't have the faith. I'm weak. My spirit is very weak. If you love me, you'll do it for me."

"Tiny ..."

"Don't ask God to forgive me. I've done it a thousand times over."

"What do you want me to pray for?"

"Ask God to take care of my family. My brother and sister and their kids. Ask him to bless them and continue to look over them."

"Okay." Simon tapped Tiny's chest.

"But most of all," Tiny sat back and allowed tears to run down his face, "please, Simon, ask God to have mercy on my soul. Ask him to have mercy on my soul. Ask him, if he will, to receive my spirit and bless me. As my friend, I want you to give me my last rites."

"Tiny ..."

"I feel death comin' for me soon, Simon. I can hear the chariots comin' for me now. I'll be dead before you get home tonight. I know it. I'll be gone."

"Tiny, I love you." Simon placed his hand on his buddy's forehead. "Close your eyes. Let's pray."

CHAPTER FOURTEEN

Three weeks had elapsed since Simon eulogized his good friend Tiny and buried him. Usually, neither rain, sleet, nor snow would prevent Simon from having Brotherhood Night. Even if only one person showed, Brotherhood Night would still go on.

But there was an exception to this rule. Tiny's cause of death was tormenting Simon. And with the plea from Tiny to warn the kids of the potential of the same thing happening to them, Simon was determined to go all-out with his next lecture. He spent two weeks promoting it. He went on local radio shows. He bought advertising space in the local papers, and he was also on a few TV programs.

The response was tremendous. Mount Vernon High School offered its gymnasium. Simon was grateful, but he refused, citing that the Boys & Girls Club was where it'd all started and that was where he preferred to have it.

Simon wanted ladies present at this particular event. He wanted successful, career-oriented, health-conscious women to be keynote speakers. Being a registered nurse, his wife, TyDixie, was chosen to be one of the keynotes.

"This is serious to me. Very serious," Simon said to Kirby while sitting behind his desk, lurking in and out of deep thought.

"What are you talking about, Brotherhood Night?"

"Yeah, I've never been as nervous or intense as I am now. I don't know what it is."

"It's the subject matter, AIDS. It's out there, big time."

"Man, I've been in prayer all week."

"Is that unusual for you?" Kirby asked playfully, trying to relax Simon.

"No, I guess it's not," Simon said lightheartedly. I guess I should just calm down some."

"I think that's a good idea."

******

Wednesday finally came, and the sun couldn't set a moment too soon. A multitude of locals and out-of-towners made their way inside the Boys & Girls Club. To help accommodate the overflowing crowd, extra bleachers were brought in as well as fold-up chairs and benches. The other rooms of the club were rigged with speakers for those not able to make it inside the gym.

Simon sat on the panel with TyDixie, Billy Thomas, James Jones, Lowes Moore, and a doctor who was a good friend and colleague of TyDixie. A green chalkboard with wheels was set up and decorated with prophylactics and birth control devices. Also propped against the chalkboard was a broom, which seemed out of place.

Simon wore a very stern expression as he walked to the podium. It didn't look like there would be any jokes told after this lecture was over. But only time would tell.

"Good evening, ladies and gentlemen, boys and girls."

"Good evening, Bruh Simon!" the enormous crowd roared back.

"We all know why we're here," Simon said in a sullen voice as he played with the change in his pocket. "Because it's Brotherhood Night, that's why we're gathered here. Usually, as you all know, this night is reserved for men. Or should I say, males. And there are times when women infiltrate the meetings. I never really minded. But this night is different. Tonight, I *want* you ... ladies to be here. Thank you for coming." The last remark was received with a round of applause.

"My wife, TyDixie, will get the chance to speak on behalf of the women and young ladies in attendance. But we should all stay and hear her because what she has to say affects men and women.

The issue I'll be speaking to you about is human relations ... sex."
Simon went over to the chalkboard and picked up the broom. "I want
you guys to understand this. I'm not encouraging you, especially not
any of you minors in here, to have sex. Particularly if you're not
married or monogamous. But if it does happen, please, please, please
protect yourself. There's a disease called AIDS out there that will kill
if you come in contact with it. And from what I've found out, you
don't have to be homosexual or an IV drug user to get it. And the
doctor here ..." Simon said and slapped his thigh. "I'm sorry, please
welcome Dr. Richard Evans. He'll explain about it further. Many of
you Mount Vernonites knew or probably heard of Little Tiny Smalls.
Well, he died from AIDS. He suffered first. Then he died. I don't want
that to happen to any of you."

Simon went on, sharing his experiences with Tiny and again
encouraging those under the sound of his voice to protect themselves
rather than wrecking themselves. He, along with Dr. Evans, gave a
demonstration of how to properly use a condom. Graphic and explicit
detail on how body fluids travel, interact, and cause infection weren't
withheld.

There were quite a few *ooohs* and *ahhhs* throughout the
demonstration. All to which Simon felt satisfaction for. That let him
know that his words were penetrating and being absorbed, not just
falling on deaf ears.

They also noted that condoms and the other forms of protection
weren't foolproof and that the safest way to protect yourself against
disease and unwanted pregnancy was abstinence.

Simon then gave the floor to TyDixie, and she took the baton.
TyDixie was more into preventive pregnancy, STDs other than AIDS,
and hygiene issues. The focus of her speech was women showing
respect for themselves and being ladylike despite their needs. In other
words, they shouldn't sell themselves short because that breeds
carelessness, and thus may bring forth an unwelcome surprise.

The night of lectures had ended, but the crowd seemed to want more knowledge. Very few, if any, left before the entire panel had their time at the mic.

In conclusion, Simon lightened up due to the encouragement and constant urging of the crowd to tell one of his trademark jokes.

"Okay, okay. One quick one," Simon acquiesced. "A man was sitting at the bar of a local speakeasy. And after every shot, he looked into his shirt pocket, then instinctively ordered another drink. He repeated the process again and again. This went on for about eight or nine times, when at last, the bartender asked him, 'Man, why do you always look inside your shirt pocket after you finish a drink?' The man looked up at him and winced. 'In my pocket here is a picture of my wife. And whenever she starts to look good to me, I'll go home.'"

The whole place—gymnasium, extra rooms, even the overflow outside—exploded with laughter. After such a tension-filled lecture program, the joke was much needed and welcomed.

"Great speech," Wanda's brother, Wesley, said as he grabbed Simon's hand and clenched it real tight.

"Thanks, I'm glad you enjoyed it." Simon yanked his hand back.

Wesley then gave Simon a menacing smile and walked away.

"Man," Kirby made his way into Simon's office, "you were great. So were the rest of the folks up there. Everybody was on point."

"Thanks." Simon took off his drenched suit jacket and placed it behind his chair. "What's that you have there?"

"Oh, this." Kirby lifted a Gatzbys Men's Clothing garment bag. "This is a new suit I bought. I have a big day tomorrow, so I decided to treat myself to a new suit."

"What's so big about tomorrow?"

"Well, first off, I have a meeting with a potential client in New Rochelle."

"Get outta here. Already?"

"Yeah, man." Kirby took a seat. "I can't take too much time off. I'll get bored. Then my head will really start bothering me."

"Don't work yourself too hard. One reason why you're not at IBM is because of your head. Take it easy. That fainting spell and collapse wasn't that long ago."

"And?" Kirby said with a sly smile, swiftly changing the subject.

"There's more?"

"I have a little dinner date with Kat tomorrow night."

Simon looked up to the ceiling and screamed, "Hallelujah." Then he grabbed Kirby and gave him the biggest bear hug. "Man, I told you, you guys would get back together."

"Whoa, Simon. It's just dinner. Just dinner."

"It's a date, right?"

"Yeah, I guess you could say that. But—"

"That's all I need to know. My prayers have been answered. Oh man, have a great time."

"Thanks, but what're you doin' tomorrow?"

"I have a few errands to run in the morning, and I'm supposed to meet with Sol in the evening."

"What for? Did he locate the missing files?"

"As a matter of fact, he didn't. But we're gonna go over some plans regarding Bennett Wilson Day."

"What's going on?"

"They, those at City Hall and the high school, are trying to see if they can do everything in one day. They feel it'll have a greater impact."

"Sounds good, but it sounds like an all-day thing to me."

"Exactly." Simon sat back down. "Hey, get on outta here. Go home and get some rest. I don't want you tired on your big day tomorrow."

"I am tired," Kirby said as the two men shook hands. "I'll call you tomorrow night."

"I hope you're not in a position to be able to, if you know what I mean." Simon gave Kirby a wink and a smile.

"Yeah, I know what you mean. I know exactly what you mean."

******

Kirby went home and didn't sleep a wink. He bubbled with excitement well into the wee hours. The thought of his first independent client meeting was enough to make him feel geeky. But his first date with Kathy since their two-year detachment was enough to make him want to do cartwheels.

The next morning, Kirby got up, showered, and shaved. His nerves were still upset, so he forewent breakfast, which was something he never did. But before going to his eleven o'clock meeting, he made a quick stop at a florist. He had two dozen long-stemmed roses delivered to Kathy at her job.

******

The meeting went extremely well with Kirby and his potential client. In fact, it went even better than Kirby expected. The gentleman agreed to hire him to set up his computer operation for his new clothing outlet.

With the day starting off on a good note, Kirby was optimistic that the night with Kathy would turn out just as good, if not better. His next destination would be his favorite barber shop in New Rochelle—Big Three Barber Shop on Main Street. This, after he bit down on a hot dog from Nathan's.

He got his hair buffed just the way he liked it. His barber, Dale Green, always knew just what to do. Now it was off to White Plains again. This time, to freshen up, change his shirt and tie, and put on a fresh coat of Kathy's favorite cologne, Polo by Ralph Lauren. His brand-new suit looked just fine on him as he modeled before the mirror at least a hundred times.

Now it was off to Metro North to catch an express train into New York City. He and Kathy were to wine and dine at Central Park's Tavern on the Green. Kathy would meet him there since she worked for a brokerage firm in midtown Manhattan.

The ride was swift and smooth, and Kirby got off at the last stop—Grand Central Station. He was sky high and unable to contain himself, so he decided to walk the ten blocks as opposed to taking a cab.

CHAPTER FIFTEEN

"Simon, where've you been?" Harry Hooch said over the phone. "Did you get my message? I've been looking all over for you."

"I just called TyDixie. She gave me the message to call you. What's up, you sound nervous?"

"I am. I've got some heavy news for you about Bennett's killer. I'm talking suspects, names, places, and reasons. This is really, really heavy. Where are you calling me from anyway? You at the club?"

"No, I'm at City Hall, the mayor's office with Sol."

"You what?"

"What's wrong, Hooch?"

"Nothing, nothing. I need you to meet me somewhere."

"Calm down, Hooch, I'll meet you. Where?"

"Meet me at the abandoned brick warehouse on Third Avenue behind the Salvation Army in two hours. It'll take me a little while to get back uptown. We should be alone there. It's deserted that time of night."

"Okay, Hooch, two hours. Let me run."

"Hey, don't mention ... Simon! Simon!"

******

When Kirby arrived, Kathy had already beaten him there, and she was seated at a table. Kirby spotted her across the room of the lavishly furnished posh restaurant, with the help of the hospitality man. She was sipping on a glass of water and was turned out in her favorite blue dress. Her hair appeared to be recently done, and it was shoulder length—just the way Kirby liked it. And she wore the pearl earrings and necklace set he'd bought her three Christmases ago. He could tell she shared the same excitement as him.

"Hi, Kat," Kirby said as the once happily married couple exchanged handshakes and kisses at the same time. "Good to see you. You look fantastic. Man, you look good."

Kathy blushed, then burst out into a soft chuckle.

"May I get you something?" the host, clad in a black and white outfit, said.

"Yes, we'll have one of your house appetizers. I don't care." Kirby put a tip into the fellow's hand without looking at him. His eyes were fixated on Kathy as he sat down. "Wow, Kathy, you really look ... good!"

"Kirby, stop ... you're embarrassing me. Besides," Kathy licked her lips seductively, "you don't look half bad yourself. In fact, you look good enough to eat."

The gesture and statement almost made Kirby choke on his water. "You hungry, Kat?" Kirby picked up the menu.

"Pretty much." Kathy picked up her own menu. "I haven't eaten anything all day."

"You either. I just had a hot dog, but it almost took me an hour to eat it."

"Kirby, you know you have to eat, and you have to take your medicine."

"Yes, Mother."

The waiter delivered the appetizers of fried shrimp and took their orders. And in a matter of minutes, the main course had come and gone.

The dessert offer was declined, but Kirby and Kathy stayed a while to chat.

"Kirby," Kathy said innocently, "what happened to us? What went wrong?"

Kirby took time to carefully configure his words before speaking. He knew how important the question was, not just for possible reconciliation, but for his mental and emotional psyche as well.

"Kat," Kirby folded his arms, "the best thing I can think of is that we married too young. I don't know if it's a good excuse, but that's how I feel. Nobody forced us to do it. We did it because we wanted to."

"Kirby, I married you straight out of high school because I fell deeply in love with you, and I wanted to spend the rest of my life with you. I wanted to have your children. I was determined to make it work and to also make a life for myself. When you joined the Navy and we had Junior, I was determined that I'd still go to college and get my degree. And when you left the Navy and enrolled in that two-year computer school, I maintained everything around the house, didn't I?"

"Yes, and you did a great job. I've always said—"

"Because to get what we both wanted out of life, I knew it would take two of us at least having decent jobs for the family to prosper. I had Bennie during my junior year of college, but I didn't miss a beat. I'm a CPA now. I have a great job. You have a great job."

"Well," Kirby corrected, "I had one."

"You know what I mean. And IBM would take you back in a flash. It's up to you and how you feel health-wise."

"Oh, Kathy," Kirby said with a trace of excitement in his voice, "I landed my first client today."

"That's great ..."

"So I doubt if I'll be going back to IBM anytime soon. Not if I can work at my own leisure and pace and still make good money."

Kathy shook her head in awe and thought of how proud she was of the man she once considered to be her soulmate. Then she offered, "How's your head? Are you still having pain?"

"No, not really. My head's fine, just fine. No stress, no tension, no real aggravation. I'm feeling pretty good."

Kathy felt the latest statement was indirectly related to her and asked, "Kirby, are you calling me aggravating?"

"Kat, where'd that come from? I was referring to my work, not you."

"So what happened to us?" Kathy asked.

"We just grew apart, that's all. I think we aged before each other's eyes. But something grew in between us. With your job and mine, I think we stopped doing the things we used to do and got comfortable with that."

Kathy let out a deep and long sigh before adding, "I hope that ... oh, nothing."

Kirby had started playing to make Kathy laugh. He was saying crazy things, making faces, and bopping his head back and forth. His attempt was met with huge success, as Kathy started tearing from laughter.

"Boy," she dotted her eyes to clear them dry, "I really miss you acting silly like Mr. T."

Kirby smiled sheepishly. "Is that all you miss?" He looked down at his lap.

"Kirby, we're in a restaurant." Kathy laughed again. This time, with a little more giggle to it.

"Hey, we're married. And the Bible states," Kirby started pointing his index finger, mimicking a preacher they both knew, "the bedroom in marriage should not be defiled."

For a second time, Kathy followed form and laughed at Kirby's statement, then added her little two cents. "It figures."

"What?"

"Here it is, you go to church maybe four times a year, but you know everything about the Bible that pertains to ..." Kathy stooped her head and lightly whispered, "sex."

"Sex!"

"Shhh, lower it down. You're a nut. Like I said, if it has something to do with marital relations, you master it."

"Hey, I gotta start somewhere, don't I."

Kathy waved her hand at him and laughed some more. She was clearly enjoying a peaceful moment that the kids wouldn't see. Then the mood turned grim as Kathy stared heavily at Kirby.

"What's wrong, Kat?"

Her eyes began to fill with water. This time, tittering hadn't preceded it. "I miss you, Kirby. I want you to come home. I want my husband back. The kids miss you something terrible."

"But I—"

"I know what you're gonna say. You spend time with them. And you do. I think you're a great father. You really are wonderful with them. But honey, I miss you, and I want you back."

Kirby blushed a little and sipped on his warm glass of water. "Kat, I miss you, too. I miss my family, too. I still love you. I still love you very much. I never stopped."

"Well," Kathy said.

"Um ... the lease is up in my apartment in two weeks, so I'll come home. I'm ready for us to be a family again. I'm ready."

"Yes! Thank you, God!" Kathy jumped over to the other side of the table to kiss on her new husband.

"Kat," Kirby tried to say in between smooches, "don't forget, we're in a restaurant, remember?"

"Oh, yeah, I almost forgot," Kathy said with her laugh coming back to her. She got off Kirby's lap, as patrons had begun staring, and took her seat again. "Baby, we'll make this work. We'll do—"

Before Kathy could go on about all she thought should happen going forward, Kirby quickly countered, "Let's just take one day at a time. Believe me, I'm just as happy about this as you are. But ... you know. One day at a time."

"Okay, I can handle it. I'm still going to be excited though."

"So, Kat," Kirby said with a sly look on his face, "when do we consummate this thing? I mean, when are you gonna ... you know ...?"

"Why did I know that was coming?"

"Hey, I'm just following procedure here. You know," Kirby started rolling his hands. "I'm just following tradition, that's all."

"That's all, huh? Well, I'd love to tonight but ..."

"Aw, don't tell me. It's that ti—"

"No, silly." Kathy looked at her watch. "After ten years of being together, and nine years of marriage, you should know that by now. I'm like clockwork, remember? You used to say that all the time."

"Yeah, yeah, but what's the problem then?"

"It's the kids. I promised Zora I'd pick them up by ten. And it's close to that now. How're we gettin' home, Kirby?"

"We'll catch a cab," Kirby said, then enquired one last time, "But can't we ...?"

"She has an early day tomorrow. Otherwise, I would. How about tomorrow? Tomorrow I'll get my mother to watch them. They can spend the night with her. And you can come over, or I'll come to your place." Kathy laughed again.

"What's so funny? This ain't no laughing matter now, Kat. This is serious. I mean real serious."

"Well, I'm laughing because I'm happy, for one. And secondly, I'm laughing because I don't believe I'm sitting here trying to arrange a tryst with my own husband."

"What, do you prefer it be someone else?"

"No, crazy. It's usually ... forget it, let's go. I love you."

"I love you, too, Kat."

CHAPTER SIXTEEN

Simon sat in his favorite spot before the window in his office, staring out into the sky pondering on his impending meeting with Harry Hooch to get more answers regarding Bennett's killer, when he was abruptly wrenched from his reverie when the door opened. His secretary stood aside to permit a woman to sweep into the room. Simon arose from his chair; the woman approached and offered her hand, which he accepted -- puzzled.

Flashes of a years-old scene coursed through his mind. She was certainly familiar. Then, he remembered.

Here was the mother of the young woman he had failed to recuse from her drug-fueled existence. How Wanda Ferguson had been treated by her own parents had always made him uncomfortable about his former protégé's death and the road that led to it. Why had her parents so little regard for their daughter? Ultimately, he had decided it wasn't his business, but now standing before him was a major player in that strange affair. Would this give him the opportunity to glean why Wanda had been estranged from her family?

"I gather you don't remember me?" She said, looking much thinner than Simon recalled.

"You're Mrs. Ferguson – Wanda's mother."

"Right . . . and I came to-to explain . . ."

"Please have a seat," Simon signaled to one of the stuffed leather chairs, and Mrs. Ferguson said down. "Would you like something to drink?"

"No."

Simon returned to his chair, sat down and rested his massive frame against the back of the chair. For a moment Mrs. Ferguson stared down at her clasped hands, then looked squarely into the face of her host.

"Wanda was my daughter . . . but not my husband Fred's daughter."

Understanding dawned to Simon, but he kept quiet.

"Fred and I were estranged, and I was at a party, where I met a guy who made me feel really special. Long story short, we slept together that night. A few months later, Fred asked to move back home. I agreed, not knowing that there were consequences to that one-night stand. When it became clear that I was pregnant, Fred knew that it could not have been his, since we weren't sleeping together at that time – I didn't deny it – I couldn't." She sighed, releasing the burden of having carried the secret for some long a period.

"He wasn't supportive, I guess."

She shook her head. "Of course not. In fact, he threw it up to me every chance he got. Even after I became pregnant with our son, he remained unforgiving. He refused to believe that it had been a moment of weakness – he chose to believe that I had probably cheated on him before, that I was a slut, and he called me that. He called me a whore whenever we argued about the least thing. If I showed even the slightest love for Wanda, he became enraged and accused me of loving another man's child more than I did our son. It wasn't true, of course, but he insisted that it was."

"I'm so sorry."

Now that the floodgates were open, they could not close again. The bitterness tripped off her tongue unbidden. "It was because he threatened to reveal my adultery to everyone that I allowed me to dictate how I responded to my daughter – and I allowed it. My heart was breaking watching my daughter become a drug addict. The fact that I could not embrace her and assure her of my love was killing me. I died when she died. That he would not allow me to give her a proper burial was the final straw. I've come back to reclaim her body and take it home to be buried with the honor she so richly deserves."

"Does he know you're here?"

"I have no idea what he knows . . . I left him, and I'm not going back. I had decided that as soon as my son was in college, I would leave, and I did."

"How can I help?"

She looked at Simon, tears cascading down her cheeks. "You've helped already. Despite my behavior you were willing to listen to me, to receive me and let me atone for my sinfulness."

"I never understood why Wanda was treated so badly by her own parents, but I knew there was more to it. Now I know, and the helplessness I always felt – the inability to save her – always haunted me. Thanks for sharing your story. I can see that you're relieved – so am I."

Mrs. Ferguson stood up. "I would like to begin a scholarship in my daughter's name – with your help.:

"Nothing would make me happier," said Simon.

******

"Harry Ho! Harry Ho! Harry Ho! Harry Hooch! Where you be, son! Come out! Come out! Wherever you are!"

A shadow of a man appeared from the darkness, but it didn't resemble Harry's body shape.

Simon became nervous and picked up a steel pipe he'd spotted on the floor. "Man, what're you doin' here? And what's the business with the gun?"

The gun was pointed toward Simon, and the chamber was cocked.

"What're you doin'? Where's Harry? Harry, you all right!"

"Save your breath. The bum is gone. Back to the dirt from whence he came. And you're about to join him."

"What? Listen, I don't want to die. Please don't." Simon said, attempting to persuade the assailant into putting the gun away.

"Why shouldn't I?"

"Man, please don't shoot me. Please," Simon begged for his life.

"I always wanted to see you sweat."

"You got it, so please let me live. Please don't kill me."

"Goodbye."

CHAPTER SEVENTEEN

Kirby reached his own home after dropping Kathy off and sharing a long kiss like the old days.

As usual, the first person he'd see upon arrival was the concierge, Antonio.

"My friend, how are you on this evening?"

"I'm feeling just great," Kirby said and gave him a tip.

"Why such a big smile? You get lucky in love?"

"Yes." Kirby's smile beamed even more. "I'm getting back with my wife, Kathy."

"Oh, so that's why so sad. You and wife separate. Me and wife together. Four children, thirty-seven years."

"Wow, thirty-seven years. That's good. I mean, great."

"When you go back?"

"My lease is up at the end of the month, and I just won't renew it."

"Me," Antonio said with a heavy Italian accent, "I retire in six months. Be finish."

"Congratulations." He shook Antonio's hand.

"You have quarter?"

"I just gave you a tip."

"No, no." Antonio held up his hands. "No tip. Take quarter out of pocket."

Kirby shook his head, as he knew not what was happening, but reached inside his pocket and took one out nonetheless.

"What year quarter?"

Kirby turned the quarter over. "1984."

"'84." Antonio reached inside his pocket. From the sound of things, you would've thought Antonio was carrying at least ten extra pounds from coins. "I have '84 also."

"Okay?"

"Let's change."

"Huh?"

"You ... me, switch quarter." Antonio snatched Kirby's away from him. "Here, take mine and put in wallet. Never spend, keep forever. I keep yours in wallet. Never spend, keep forever. Whenever I see quarter, I think of you. Never forget."

"Okay ... that'll work. Friends forever, I like that." Kirby shoved the quarter into a compartment in his wallet.

Antonio grabbed the unsuspecting Kirby, and the two men hugged. "I'll miss you, my friend. I'll miss very much my friend forever."

"Take good care of yourself, Antonio."

Before he knew it, Kirby was back upstairs. He was so excited about going home again that he started packing his clothes. When he was just about to turn it in for the evening, he was greeted with a phone call.

"TyDixie," a suddenly frightened Kirby said. "What's wrong?"

"It's Simon, he's not home yet, and it's well past 2:00 a.m. I'm worried. He'd never stay out this late without calling."

"Doesn't sound like him. Doesn't sound like him at all."

"I'm sorry for calling you this late."

"Please TyDixie. It's not a problem." Kirby searched for his shoes. "I'd be angry if you hadn't. Did he say where he was going last?"

"I know he told me he had to meet with that Harry Hooch guy."

"Oh, you mean, Hairy Hooch?"

TyDixie slightly laughed before she answered, "Yeah, him. He said Harry had some serious information to give him. I didn't ask him what it was, but it sounded real important. Maybe I'm just a little paranoid. Maybe they're just out having a good time, and he lost track of the time. But I'm worried, Kirby. I'm worried."

"That's okay, I am as well." Kirby re-snapped his pants. "But did Simon say or give a hint as to where he was going to meet with him? And where was he when you last spoke?"

"When he called me last, he was at the mayor's office." TyDixie then paused for a moment to think and get her bearings. "I believe I heard him say something about the Salvation Army. I don't know if that makes any sense or not."

Kirby pondered the thought for several seconds. "Salvation Army, Salvation Army ... Third Avenue ...warehouse. Did he say something about a warehouse?"

"It sounds—"

"TyDixie, I'll call you back when I find him. Just sit tight."

Kirby hung up in a flash, snatched on his suit jacket, and headed out the door for his car. He must've shattered every speed law on the Hutchinson Parkway and ran every red light from White Plains to Mount Vernon. The good Lord was with him because no cops were around at the time of his Mario Andretti impersonation.

Kirby arrived at his destination and noticed Simon's car amidst the darkness and fog. He became nervous as he picked up a brick and headed toward the building. He jumped in fear as a cat whisked pass him. It was clean and didn't resemble any of Harry Hooch's cats.

"Simon! Simon! Can you hear me! Are you there!"

Kirby walked around some more until he noticed a foul smell in the air. He looked down and saw Harry—his head bleeding, and his eyes bugged open.

"Harry! Goodness gracious!" Kirby reached down. He took Harry's hand and pressed on a vein in Harry's neck to see if he was still alive.

There was no pulse. Harry was dead.

"I gotta find Simon." Kirby ran, having no clue where he was headed in the darkened passageway. He just wanted to find his friend. He wanted to be able to call TyDixie and tell her Simon was all right, that he'd found him.

Kirby's steady pace was interrupted when he suddenly lost his footing on something slippery. He went two feet in the air and landed on his back. On impact, the brick flew out of his hand. Kirby, slightly dazed, got up and looked around to see what had befallen him. His eyes wouldn't tell him though because the darkness was too great. That's when he saw Simon, lying on the ground.

"Simon!" Kirby ran toward him. "You all right?"

There was no answer from Simon as he bled from the chest and shoulder area. Kirby cradled him in his arms to comfort him, and he felt for a pulse.

"Bennett—who—oh, God—I mean, Simon, who did this to you?" Kirby's head throbbed as the pressure of seeing his good friend suffering became too great.

The thought of having seen Bennett the same way made matters even worse.

"Simon, don't die on me, man. Keep your eyes open. Man, fight back! Simon! You better not die on me! You're bleeding all over my brand-new suit. Fight, man!"

Kirby instinctively started searching around for help that he knew wasn't there.

"Oh, God, please don't let him die now. He has a family, a wife and a little girl. Please," Kirby cried and cradled Simon tighter.

"Yeah, Simon, keep your eyes open," he said, still rocking back and forth. "I have a joke for you. Simon, listen to me. Keep your eyes open. A guy went home and found his wife packing her suitcase. He asked, 'Where do you think you're going?'

"'Las Vegas,' she replied. 'I hear out there I can make three hundred dollars every time I have sex.' The guy ran into the other bedroom and started packing his own suitcase.

"'And where are you goin'?' his wife asked.

"'Las Vegas. I wanna see how you can live on six hundred dollars a year.'"

Through the midst of his agony, Simon managed a feeble smile.

"Come on, Simon, keep your eyes open," Kirby pleaded when he saw Simon's eyes roll back as he went into a convulsion. "Oh, God, please!" Kirby placed Simon down on the ground. He then ripped off his jacket and laid it under Simon's head. He took off his shirt and put it under Simon's left shoulder.

Kirby spotted a ray of light and figured it was an entranceway. It was, so he made a break for it. "Help! Help! Help! Somebody! Somebody shot Simon! Help! Somebody! Call an ambulance! Please! Somebody, help! Somebody, call for help! Please!"

THE END

ESSAY QUESTIONS

1. Who do you think shot Bennett?
2. Imagine you are Kirby, how do you feel about your life, now and then?
3. This should be a well-known fact by now, but what do the letter A.I.D.S mean?
4. How can it affect the life of an individual?
5. Did it change the way the way Simon felt toward his friend, Little Tiny Smalls?
6. In what way did Bennett's little brother Dannon remind Kirby of him?
7. Do you think Kirby and Simon were truly friends?
8. What landed Simon in prison?
9. Did prison do Simon any good?
10. How did Kirby feel regarding young teenaged girls getting pregnant?
11. When Kirby confronted Sol while he was mayor, how did he feel?
12. Besides Midnight Basketball, what is another solution to keep young people off the streets?

TOPICS OF DISCUSSION

1. The importance of a good relationship between PARENT and CHILD.

2. The importance of FAIR play; going through life without having to cheat.

3. Saying "NO" to drugs.

4. Saying "NO" to alcohol.

5. Saying "NO" to guns.

6. The importance of having the RIGHT kind of friends.

7. The ability to realize that you are you own person, and not let peer pressure become an endangerment to you.

8. Make every day count toward working at a positive goal.

9. The importance of staying in school.

10. The significance of striving to avoid unplanned teen-age pregnancy.

www.TheHeroBookSeries.com

Made in USA - North Chelmsford, MA
1060779_9781717437518
03.23.2020 1131